THE HEART CHANGER

Only *He* Could Set a Captive Free

Ambassador International
GREENVILLE, SOUTH CAROLINA & BELFAST, NORTHERN IRELAND

www.ambassador-international.com

"A captivating story that weaves characters together from a volatile time in Israel's history to reveal the power of faith and forgiveness. Young hearts will find hope to face their perplexing and changeable world."

—TINA CHO,
author of *Rice From Heaven*

"*The Heart Changer* is a touching tale of loss, faith, and healing. Jarm Del Boccio spins together vivid details that bring Miriam's world to life. Her story is sure to capture readers' hearts."

—CARMELA A. MARTINO,
author of the award-winning novel *Playing by Heart*

THE HEART CHANGER

Only *He* Could Set a Captive Free

JARM DEL BOCCIO

AMBASSADOR INTERNATIONAL
GREENVILLE, SOUTH CAROLINA & BELFAST, NORTHERN IRELAND

www.ambassador-international.com

The Heart Changer

© 2019 by Jarmila V. Del Boccio

ISBN: 978-1-62020-868-7
eISBN: 978-1-62020-889-2
Library of Congress Control Number: 2019932466

Scripture taken from the King James Version (KJV). Public Domain.

Cover Design & Typesetting by Hannah Nichols
Ebook Conversion by Anna Riebe Raats
Edited by Ashley Wallace

AMBASSADOR INTERNATIONAL
Emerald House
411 University Ridge, Suite B14
Greenville, SC 29601, USA
www.ambassador-international.com

AMBASSADOR BOOKS
The Mount
2 Woodstock Link
Belfast, BT6 8DD, Northern Ireland, UK
www.ambassadormedia.co.uk

The colophon is a trademark of Ambassador, a Christian publishing company.

Dedication

To my daughter, Olivia, whose stubborn heart was softened at the age of seven by the Heart Changer. She, too, traveled many miles before reaching our hearts and home. You are my grown-up Miriam!

A Heartfelt Thanks

To my mini beta readers, Lydia, Grace and Elizabeth (and their mom), whose cartwheeling near the Syrian Desert made me realize your daily life is much like Miriam's. Thank you for your input on life and culture in the Middle East. I know your delightful spirits bring joy to captive hearts.

To Alice Herzig and her Messianic Jewish husband Steve, with The Friends of Israel Gospel Ministry staff—your insights on the Jewish culture and language have been invaluable. I love your editor's heart, Alice!

To my critique partner, Sarah Glenn Fortson, who loved Miriam's story from the start and gave helpful edits for the opening chapter. Your time has come!

To Ashley Wallace, my editor, who made the revision process challenging but enjoyable. Thanks to Ambassador International's COO, Anna Raats, for keeping me on track. Your knowledge of the publishing business and social media is remarkable. To Hannah Nichols, my creative director, whose unending patience touched me as I made multiple suggestions and changes for the cover and text of my novel. What a receptive and willing heart!

To my hubby Dan, whose generous heart has given me the space, a place, and grace to become the writer I'm meant to be.

And how can I not give thanks to my Savior, the Lord Jesus Christ, for inspiring me to write Miriam's story? He is still in the process of changing my willful and selfish heart. To Him be the glory!

Lastly, I look forward to the day when I can sit down with the real-life Miriam in Heaven and discover how close I was to the truth!

Create in me a clean heart, O God; and renew a right spirit within me.

Psalm 51:10 (KJV)

The Master Weaver

Our lives are but fine weavings
That God and we prepare,
Each life becomes a fabric planned
And fashioned in His care.
We may not always see just how
The weavings intertwine,
But we must trust the Master's hand
And follow His design,
For He can view the pattern
Upon the upper side,
While we must look from underneath
And trust in Him to guide . . .

Sometimes a strand of sorrow
Is added to His plan,
And though it's difficult for us,
We still must understand
That it's He who fills the shuttle,
It's He who knows what's best,
So we must weave in patience
And leave to Him the rest . . .

Not till the loom is silent
And the shuttles cease to fly
Shall God unroll the canvas
And explain the reason why —
The dark threads are as needed
In the Weaver's skillful hand
As the threads of gold and silver
In the pattern He has planned.

—Author Unknown

CHAPTER ONE

"RUN! RUN, MY DAUGHTER! DON'T let them see you!" Miriam's mother cried in alarm, shielding baby Zacchaeus in her long robes. She watched, helpless, as her precious child ran to escape the oncoming invasion.

Picking up her skirts, the young girl fled down the center of the Shunem town market, following the frantic path of others, terror-stricken by the billowing clouds of dust gathering in the distance. As the villagers ran for their lives, baskets of fruits and vegetables, nuts and spices were carelessly scattered on the parched ground. Carts of fish and goat's cheese were upset, the sound of splintering and cracking adding to the mayhem as striped awnings ripped from their doorframes. Goats and sheep scattered, and those who could not be freed from their leads bleated in fear. Shouts of the Syrian army, and the sound of clomping horses' hooves on the stone pavement signaled the enemy's advance. Cries and screams escaped from the villagers as they dropped a trail of precious belongings in their flight. A keepsake and a fresh loaf of bread meant nothing. Only their lives mattered now.

Miriam eyed another overturned cart, its sweets scattered in the dust, and swiftly darted behind it to evade the soldiers' haunting advances. She covered her face with the cloth from her head covering, tucking it in to hide her maturing face. Heart pounding, she took a deep breath, pressing her head against the rugged wood, praying no one had seen her. At twelve, who knew what the enemy would do if they caught her? Miriam shuddered as she heard the screams of women and children running past. She wiped her palms and forehead with the hem of her skirts, and shut her eyes tightly, trying to block out the horrifying scene.

"Oh—Jehovah—help!" she pleaded, gasping with each word. "ALL of us. Mother—Father—and—baby Zacchaeus. Shield us—from our—enemies."

"Miriam!"

Recognizing a familiar voice, Miriam instinctively stood up, just as a soldier galloped towards her. Miriam froze, unable to avoid the oncoming danger. Her heart beat wildly, mouth gaping as she watched in seemingly slow motion the muscular legs of the horse moving in rhythm in her line of vision, hooves kicking up the dust as they beared down, threatening to trample her. As the soldier galloped by, she felt herself being lifted off the ground, and in one smooth movement, flung onto the front of the beast, knocking the wind from her lungs.

Miriam coughed forcefully, then drew in a deep breath, reaching for the only thing within her grasp — the horse's mane. Her legs flapped against the equine's flank, as the soldier's sweaty arms encircled her. Dizzy from the rapid motion, Miriam closed her eyes, confused momentarily by shouts and screams mingled with the sound of crashing and thuds.

"Trying to hide, eh?" the soldier said with a cruel laugh.

The horse and rider took a turn at the main street of town and headed towards the open expanse of countryside, a trail of other soldiers racing behind. As the village disappeared in the distance, the sounds of terror and defeat turned to victorious whoops and cheers. The rough bouncing of the horse's gallop shook the delicately framed young girl until hot tears flowed down Miriam's cheeks. The dust from the road enveloped her, sticking to her tears so she could barely see. Anger rose within her soul.

"Where—?" Miriam demanded, her voice jagged and bouncy. "Let me—my Mo—"

"You will see—and it will bring me a pretty drachma." He shouted over the clatter of hooves and gathering soldiers on their own steeds, then laughed heartily. Miriam tried to block it out by squeezing her eyes shut, as if they were ears.

Why, Jehovah? Miriam poured out her grief in a series of sobs, not caring what her captor thought. Exhausted, she hung her head, her shoulders slumping, while still managing to hang on. The images of women and children running for their lives played over and over in her mind, her ears still ringing with their screams. When would this nightmare end?

It seemed like hours since they left the scene of the invasion. By now, the sun was setting, casting its vibrant coral-colored rays onto the parched ground. Miriam could see through greasy strands of hair, smoke rising in the distance. She desperately hoped it was a camp. With each bounce Miriam grimaced, her legs aching from hanging on. Her entire frame felt heavy, each muscle and bone jostling, begging for rest.

"I can't." Miriam said in a weak, raspy voice. "I can't stand any more. Too tired."

The rider slowed his horse as he came to a group of other soldiers eating around a fire, coarse jesting and hollow laughs echoing across the desert. They were throwing bones from their stew at one another, and as they landed in the fire, or hit a head, laughter pealed once more.

"Where is the commander?" Miriam's captor demanded.

"In the tent, Galius." The men fixed their gazes on Miriam. She immediately turned away, burying her face in her sleeve.

"Part of the spoils, eh?" a soldier observed.

"Stop it. She's a gift to the commander."

Galius led his horse away from the army's tents, stopping by a post to secure its reins alongside the other soldier's horses, allowing them to rest and graze. He dismounted first, then grabbing hold of Miriam's robe at the shoulder dragged her to the ground.

"I won't tie your hands—walk alongside—you won't get hurt. Understand?" he said in halting Hebrew.

She did. Clearly. *I am now a slave.* Miriam nodded with her head still bowed, in response. *What will happen to me? Will I ever see home again? What about—*She dared not think of them. Miriam's thoughts continued to plague her as her feet kick up the dust and random stones in the path. This day started with so much hope. Now despair covered her like a heavy cloak, hiding any chance of redemption.

CHAPTER TWO

THEY CAME TO THE ENTRANCE of a large tent, adorned with brilliant scarlet, green and yellow patterned silks. A flame burned inside a piece of pottery that had an open carved design to let the light shine through. A tall, dark, broad-shouldered man dressed in a short brown tunic with a gold sash met them. Miriam's gaze left the ground and moved to his sandaled feet laced up his muscular calves, then past his tunic to his face. He towered over her, but barely noticed her existence, glancing down once or twice as he spoke in that strange tongue.

"Yes, Galius? What is it? I'm busy with preparations for our return home."

"Commander, sir?"

"Yes—quickly now."

"I have captured a girl from our raid on Shunem as you have requested. I spied her just as she was about to run across my path. I think she is perfect for the task, sir."

The man in charge looked down once more. This time he studied the subject of their conversation.

"Turn around, girl." He motioned circling his finger.

Miriam obeyed. Thankfully, the walk in the cool evening air was enough to waken her tired frame. The commander examined her carefully, putting his forefinger on his chin and rested it there.

"Hmmmmm. I suppose . . ."

"She's quick," said the soldier, "—and agile."

"Yes, but will she be able to follow commands without question?"

"That I cannot say, sir."

"Well, girl?" Miriam startled and looked up when she heard her native language.

"Are you willing to be obedient in my household? Can you serve my wife well? She wants a hard-working girl, not a lazy one." The commander looked directly into Miriam's eyes.

Her thoughts raced as her eyes remained focused on the commander. Deep rugged lines traced his dark angular face. His jaw set, waiting for a response. *He looks like an important man. Better him than another. And maybe—someday—he will let me go home.*

Uncertainty rose inside her, but she quickly squashed it. Boldness fought for first place and won. She stood erect and spoke slowly but clearly.

"Yes, sir, I can serve your wife. I cared for my baby brother while my ima gained her strength after birthing. My abba says I am the brightest star in our village. And I turned twelve last month." She raised her chin betraying a tiny trace of pride.

Without comment, the commander said, "Take her to the women's tent and give her something to eat. She will do."

He waved them towards a large tent, with smoke wafting from a fire in front of its entrance. Miriam's stomach growled as she took in the aroma of roasted meat. Lamb? Then, in horror, she thought: *The commander is a Gentile. He knows nothing of our ways. Could the smell be that of—of—pig?*

"Come with me," the soldier spoke abruptly.

Half of her wanted to flee. The other half was hungry. Miriam turned her body swiftly, wrenching her cloak from his grasp.

"Oh, no you don't. Not now—now the commander has approved you."

He grasped her robe again; this time, tighter. He led her to the small enclosure with a well-worn tent. A few women and children sat around the blazing fire, warming themselves from the effects of the cool evening. A pot of stew boiled on top. Miriam's stomach began to growl again.

"Take care of her. We have plans for this one." Galius pushed her towards the group and locked the enclosure behind him.

A young girl, close to Miriam's age, with dark tangled hair and a dirty tunic stepped out of the tent. Her bright smile seemed out of place. But Miriam recognized her immediately—a Shunammite girl.

"What—How? Joanna!"

She ran to Miriam and embraced her. "Oh, Miriam. Jehovah has sent you to me. I was praying I would see a friendly face."

"Back into the tent!" snarled a woman bending at the fireside. She was wrapped in sooty clothing, her bony finger pointing at the opening.

"I must go. We will talk later."

The girl disappeared immediately into the tent as directed. Miriam felt hopeful for the first time since she was ripped from her beloved town. She pulled her now dirty and ragged cloak closely around her. It felt safe.

"Come. Have some stew." The older woman beckoned her, holding out a steaming bowl.

She inched towards the provisions, stomach growling. Then she wavered. *Will Jehovah forgive me for eating an unclean animal? Surely, He won't care if a starving captive takes a bite of pig, will He?*

"Quickly girl. I can't hold it all evening." The haggard woman shoved the bowl towards her, this time, sloshing some of the stew over the rim. "See what you made me do?"

Miriam grabbed it and moved back.

"If you are going to be fit for the commander's family, stay away from that girl. She will be no help." The woman motioned back towards the open tent flap.

Miriam ignored the woman and walked towards the fence. She leaned against it, face toward the setting sun. Squinting, she tried to recall the events of the day. Where were her parents? And baby Zacchaeus? Would there be anything left of her beloved home if she were freed someday? *Oh, Abba in heaven, please hear my prayer.* Tears mixed with rain fell into her stew. The cold night air wrapped itself around her tired body. She shivered, then ate quietly, chewing slowly as she savored each morsel, thankful she had a meal to calm her grumbling belly.

CHAPTER THREE

THE NEXT MORNING, AFTER A night of tossing and turning, Miriam awoke bleary-eyed and exhausted, her body resisting to rise. She turned on her side and pushed herself off the cold, hard ground and moaned. Sitting up, she rubbed her temples trying to soothe her headache and erase yesterday's memories. Impossible. She could barely will herself to live, let alone, move on. The heartache was far worse than her headache.

Will I ever see my little brother again? Was my ima taken, too? And my dear abba? The questions swirled in her head like flies, causing her head to throb even more.

Miriam and the other captives were led east on foot across the Jordan River through Ramoth-Gilead and beyond. The desert was unforgiving. The ground was parched, the air dry, and the day hot with the sun beating down on the line of captives which seemed to go on for miles. Whatever breeze there was, blew swirling sand into mouths and eyes, and tossed loose bramble bushes across the desert, rolling so fast, Miriam imagined they were being chased by an enemy.

Her body, sore from resting on the hard ground, made the grueling journey even more difficult. The bit of hummus she was given for breakfast hardly satisfied her appetite. Miriam longed for her mother's goat's cheese and flatbread. She imagined waking to the aroma of baking bread on hot stones that filled their dwelling each morning. How she missed it!

The captives suddenly slowed their pace. Miriam peered into the distance, shielding her eyes from the glaring sun. *Water!* Miriam couldn't believe her eyes. She slowed down, impatiently creeping forward like a tortoise. *Finally.* Stepping into the cool, refreshing Jordan, her tired feet immediately gained strength. What was it about water that renewed body and spirit? She observed the effects on others around her. As the women raised their skirts to avoid dampening them, children jumped and played. Everyone, Miriam included, dipped their cupped hands into the river and drank lustily. She thought she heard laughter, too.

"Miriam! Wait!" A voice called from behind. She turned and saw her Shunammite friend trudging forward, the water slowing her stride. "I'm so happy to find you! I know not a soul among the captives—I was lonely."

"Joanna!" Miriam moved to her side and embraced her. "Oh, it is *so* good to see a familiar face!" she said, pushing her back at arm's distance, studying Joanna's face. She was puzzled to see a smile.

"How can you be happy, Joanna? After all that has happened? I could never . . ." Her voice trailed off as she watched captive after captive, shoulders hunched, head bowed, pressing onward. *And for what purpose?*

"Miriam. We can't know why this happened. Only Jehovah in His wisdom knows. But—we must be faithful."

"*Faithful?* To the All-Powerful One who could have stopped this?" Clenching her fists Miriam said, "Look at us! They had no right to take us from our homes. To burn our village. To kill our people. I *hate* them!"

"Oh, Miriam. Jehovah would not want you to hate. Do not say that."

"But it is true. We have done *nothing* to deserve this. *Nothing!*" she cried in a harsh whisper to avoid drawing attention. "And what of your family? Where are they?"

Joanna hung her head. "They—they were—they are dead."

Miriam bristled in anger, her face reddening. "And you think we have no right to hate? You, of all people, should hate them!"

"No, I don't. I can't. It is His will." Joanna raised her right hand to the sky and looked up, as if Heaven would open.

"His will? Jehovah would *will* this?" Miriam shook her fists at the sky.

A shout came from behind.

"You. Maids. Stop! You will be in more trouble than you are now."

They turned to see the old woman who sat by the fire the night before. Her face held a scowl that wouldn't let go. The girls immediately waded more quickly, then reached the shore. Their sandals dripped onto the sand, causing clumps that stuck to the sides. Wringing out the hem of their skirts, the two continued their conversation.

"Is she in charge?" Miriam asked. "Why does she show such interest in us?"

Joanna answered her curiosity. "She is given extra food for making sure the choicest slaves are cared for. I am not one, of course, but you are. She is watching out for you."

"Oh. I see. Because I am going to be the servant of—" She stopped abruptly and then went on. "Who is this man anyway? Why is he so important?"

"You don't know? Why, he is Naaman, the commander of all the armies in Syria, and has won a great many wars for King Ben-Hadad. He is a mighty warrior, Miriam."

"So, I should be the servant of the wife of the man who destroyed my village? My people? And maybe, my—"

"Yes, Miriam. It seems Jehovah has willed it."

"But I . . . ."

"Move. Get going—no talking." A soldier on horseback trotted past, barking orders, his horse kicking up clods of mud. One struck Miriam in the shoulder. Fuming, she flung it to the ground and grimaced. She looked up at Joanna, who continued with a peaceful countenance. Miriam sighed, then offered her friend a crooked smirk.

Fearing consequences, but loathed to part, the girls obeyed, but not before they shared a bittersweet smile, locking hands and eyes for only a moment.

The day wore on, heat rising from the surface of the parched ground, as the march through the desert continued. Their feet blistered with the heat radiating through their ragged sandals. Their brows dripped with sweat, tongues sticking to the roof of their mouths. The long procession progressed as the captives trudged along, heads lowered, resigned to their destiny. They didn't care. They didn't talk. They just moved forward. Forward to who knows where. Only the all-knowing Jehovah knew.

And where was the Almighty anyway, when our village was attacked?

CHAPTER FOUR

MIRIAM KEPT HER THOUGHTS TO herself as they limped towards an unknown destination. The path led on with no end in sight, stretching out towards the now reddening horizon. In her mind, she beckoned the image of her hometown before the attack. Miriam imagined walking to the well on a scorching day. It was not one of her favorite tasks, but now, she wished for nothing more. To go back and be the big sister. To look after Zacchaeus. To embrace her ima and abba. She took so much for granted, and now—well, for all she knew, they were lost. Maybe even dead. A tear trailed down her cheek, but she brushed the intruder away with her dust-laden sleeve.

By the end of the sweltering hot day, after miles and miles of barren flat land to cross, the soldiers stopped the hoard from advancing and settled under a small grove of palm trees. Having nowhere but the dusty hard ground to lay their tired bodies, the captives were thankful for the rest. Miriam looked up at the night sky, the full moon brilliant against the open expanse of the heavens, surrounded by a multitude of stars.

She thought she saw them twinkle as if alive and imagined them winking as her abba did when he showed his pride in her obedience. Miriam cringed, thinking of the times she obeyed on the outside, but held stubbornness in her heart. *I'm sorry dear abba. Will you ever—?* Hot tears flowed again with the realization she might never see him again.

"Jehovah, please—let them be safe. I'll try to be good. Please." Miriam spoke to a silent night sky. She closed her moist eyes and fell asleep, exhausted from the day's wearisome journey.

The next morning, at sunrise, the soldiers rounded up the captives, their whips snapping the earth as they yelled their orders. For nourishment, bags of dried dates and apricots were left for the taking along with a goatskin of water to pass amongst them as they prepared for the trek ahead.

Flat ground, covered with sand rippling from the wind was replaced by sand dunes dotting the landscape along the route, as they moved forward, side by side. Soon, tamarisk trees appeared, their full form sporting tiny white to pink flowers. Miriam took a deep breath, calmed by the changing landscape. It seemed to suddenly change from bare desert brown to vibrant green in a matter of a few miles. What was once flat land became gently rolling hills covered with vegetation.

On the horizon, a city slowly came into view, spreading across the uninhabited greening desert. The multi-leveled stone structures seemed to rise from the dust as a grove of towering palms reaching out towards the sky. Eyes wide and mouth paused open in wonder, Miriam gawked at the scene before her, taking it all in from her place in line. *Where are we? What is this place?*

As they were driven forward, the buildings in the walled city grew until they overshadowed the mass of captives, blocking out the sun. Murmurs rose as they craned their necks to take in the massive stone gate before them. The arch itself, the entry to the city, was taller and wider than any home Miriam had seen in her entire life. She studied the relief symbols carved into the wall of the entrance—a pair of wings stretched out with no body, and a circle, like the sun where a head would lie. Over the arch was a four petaled flower reaching in four directions inside a circle. Two enormous pillars with decorative caps graced each side of the arch.

Miriam could hear the mumbling, chatter and shouts of the citizens inside. A gatekeeper dressed in a regimental red and gold tunic met their captors who had maneuvered in front of the line with their horses. After a brief conversation, the wooden gates were opened to allow them entrance. One of their soldiers stopped his horse at the gate as the others paraded forward with the Syrian battle flag flying high.

"Move along," he ordered. "Stay in single file. Go!"

Miriam advanced with the others, wondering what she would find in this magnificent city. For a few moments, she was overcome. Men and women and children strolled in fine silk clothing; men with turbans and women with long colorful fabrics with elegant flowered designs wrapped around their heads and trailing down their backs. Street vendors lined the straight, wide main street on either side, selling fruits, vegetables, herbs and spices foreign to a mere village girl. Baskets, brilliant fabrics and weavings, along with fine pottery were displayed—Miriam was dizzy with it all!

As they walked, some of the captives tripped as they slowed their pace to stare. Men on camels lumbered alongside them, with parcels filled with goods. Up ahead, Miriam could see what she thought to be a temple to foreign gods. Elaborate tiles and mirrored surfaces in square and triangular patterns adorned the facade—it was all overwhelming.

Miriam forgot her plight and became lost in her surroundings. Everything was new and exciting. She took a deep breath of spice-scented air. Familiar scents of cumin, oregano, and thyme mixed with the sweet smells of coriander, cardamom, and cinnamon made her mouth water. How she wished she could have a sip of her ima's sweet goat's milk tea, her special remedy for a queasy stomach.

Hope began to rise in her heart. *Maybe I can find someone to help me. Someone to help me get back to my village. Back to my family.*

But, it wasn't to be.

The captives were driven to the end of the street called Straight, where an expansive open marketplace was located. In the center sat a single large stone platform. Men in brown leather tunics with scraggly beards and angry faces waited with whips, their gruff voices ordering the soldiers to lead their captives to the platform. Motioning to the chains embedded into the rock, they commanded the soldiers to secure the hands and feet of the women and children. One by one, the women, and children were placed on the platform for all to examine. To gawk.

To her horror, Miriam suddenly realized what was happening. Her head began to spin, her heart pounding in her chest. Her mouth went dry as the smell of sweat mixed with the heat of the day, and the wailing of the captives hit her. *Nooooo!* Miriam held her breath, as she moved forward, thankful she was last. Suddenly, she was jerked out of line. It was Galius.

"Where do you think you are going?" He grabbed her tunic and pulled her alongside. "We have plans for you."

Miriam tugged back, but it was no use. The soldier won this battle. She obediently complied, at least with her body. However, her spirit put up a fight. *I will not be treated like this. I will show them. They can't do this to me.*

Miriam's short gait was no match for Galius' long stride, so it was a struggle for her to keep up. She breathed heavily, taking in the dust from the ground. It almost choked her. They soon stopped alongside a glistening chariot, carved with gold rosettes. She noticed the commander waiting there. Shielding her eyes from the sun's rays, Miriam bravely fixed her gaze on his face, her hands forming a tight fist. Naaman's forehead furrowed. His eyes fixed on hers. Miriam watched as the corners of his mouth upturned ever so slightly.

Heat rose in her chest and threatened to escape in a torrent of words. *How dare he do this to my people?*

"Thank you, Galius. Well done." The commander congratulated the soldier with a firm slap on the shoulder. "She will be perfect. Adara has been asking for a young maiden to assist her with household tasks since harvest time last year. This one looks strong, but intelligent."

The comment took Miriam by surprise. *Me?*

Naaman raised her into his chariot with care, catching her off-guard. *Just like my abba. How can he be so kind, after what he has done?* He climbed up beside her and grabbed the reins and slapped the two horses with the leather straps, lurching them forward.

Miriam cried out, grabbing the edge of the chariot tightly with her fingers as it jostled on the rutted street. *I will not be afraid. I will be strong. I—*

"Not accustomed to riding in a chariot, eh?" The commander chuckled lightly and continued to direct his entourage of soldiers behind him, their banners flying high. Making their way down the main thoroughfare, they navigated the marketplace stalls on the way out of town. The merchants stopped their bargaining and stood tall, saluting their mighty warrior. She felt small and insignificant standing beside him. Other onlookers turned to bow in respect as the wheels of the chariot clacked down the stone pavement, drawing attention to its occupants. Some folks stood wide-eyed with their mouths agape.

Others furrowed their brows, heads cocked in puzzlement. "She is so young!" observed one, shaking his head. "It's a shame war touches such an innocent girl," said another, loud enough for Miriam to hear.

Her melancholy thoughts turned back to those being auctioned as slaves in the marketplace. *It could have been me.*

Soon the expanse of land opened up as they headed towards a small range of hills. The day was coming to a close, the evening sky layered in brilliant crimson, yellow golds and burnt oranges. Miriam drew in a deep breath, head tilted heavenward, her body still in quiet adoration. But, all at once, the worries of the day returned as quickly as they vanished.

How can a beautiful sunset appear when my future is dark and colorless? Is Jehovah really here with me in enemy territory? Most likely, He was towering over the earth, allowing things to happen by chance. But, no—what about Ruth the Moabite? She was a refugee like me, far from home. Her husband was dead. She had no children. But didn't Jehovah turn it all around? She chose to follow Naomi's God, the Lord Jehovah, even in the face of trials. Will my life turn out someday as brilliant as the heavens?

Miriam looked up at the sky searching for an answer. *There's no hope for me. The heavens are silent tonight.*

CHAPTER FIVE

EVEN THOUGH THE RIDE WAS not as rough as she expected, Miriam's eyes watered as she gripped the edge of the chariot, the muscles on her thighs screaming for rest. Just then, the chariot slowed and stopped in front of a large edifice. Its imposing massive grey stones seemed to swallow her, stealing her breath. Miriam felt twice a captive now. An iron gate, decorated with twists of rosettes and curved swirling lines, opened at the Commander's call by a servant dressed in a red and bronze tunic.

"Welcome home, Commander Naaman, sir. Glad to see you have arrived safely." He glanced at the young girl in the chariot, his eyes widening. But, his countenance relaxed with an understanding nod, as if remembering Naaman's promise to his wife.

"Thank you, Ahmad. It is good to be back. Is the mistress of the house present?"

"Yes, sir. She is resting. Shall I tell her you desire to see her?"

"No. I want to surprise her. Take the chariot and tend to the horses."

Naaman jumped down from the chariot and swung around to help Miriam down. She grabbed the edge of her tunic ready to lift the hem to prevent her foot from stepping on it and ripping. As she turned her head, Miriam noticed a beautiful young girl peeking from behind the entrance gate, dressed in fine sky-blue silk with a headband holding a precious azure jewel which rested on her forehead. Miriam couldn't take her eyes off this gentle but fine-looking figure.

"Come . . . uh . . . what is your name? I never asked."

Miriam turned back quickly towards the commander, embarrassed by her distracted posture. "Miriam. Miriam, sir." She wasn't sure what to call him, either.

As if he could read her mind he said, "You may call me, Master Naaman. And my wife, Mistress Adara." Miriam nodded and allowed the master to help her off the chariot.

"And that," motioning to the young girl, "is Vashti. She is full of curiosity, that daughter of mine." He winked at Vashti, and immediately the young girl rushed to his side.

"Baba! It's so good to have you home—we've missed you." She giggled gently, hugging her father. Miriam thought her smile was charming and her laughter like a musical waterfall.

The Master turned and said, "Come, Miriam. Let me show you to the mistress of the house. She will be pleased—I know."

There was something gentle about the commander which puzzled Miriam. How could he lead an army to war, kill and take captive hundreds of people, and yet speak warmly to her? She wasn't sure how to respond. *If my family has been killed, I will never forgive the master. It's all his fault. But, what if they are safe? He is the only one that could help me find them.* Miriam didn't know whether to pull away and scream, telling him she wanted to go home, or meekly go with him. She chose the latter for now.

They made their way down the cool stone hall, Miriam's dusty sandals slapping against the cobbled surface. A shiver escaped her weary body. A soft humming drifting into the corridor—one unfamiliar but beautiful nonetheless. Sounds of bubbling water soothed her spirits.

As they walked through an archway, Miriam's eyes rested on a woman lounging on a couch, the glow of the setting sun surrounding her like a tiara. She stopped humming and looked up. First, a questioning frown, then, a slowly spreading smile filled her face. But Miriam noticed only her striking green eyes. Never before had she seen such a color. For a moment, they brought a breath of life and peace.

"Oh. I thought it was that bothersome servant again. She just can't leave me alone for a minute. How are you my dear? Did the battle go well?" The woman spoke matter-of-factly, as though nothing out of the ordinary had happened.

Miriam felt her body tense, her chest tightening. *Yes, the battle went well, my dear. Killed as many men, women, and children as we could in the little village and took this one for your pleasure.*

Naaman's wife reached out her long, slender chestnut arms towards the master. "And, who is this?" She turned her head, decked with jewels and gold cord woven through her thick raven hair, and gave Miriam an impish grin. She beckoned her with a graceful gesture.

If everything is to go well, and I plan to find my family again, I had better behave. Be wise, Miriam. She forced a smile, and walked forward, bowing her head slightly. "I am Miriam, Mistress. My name is Miriam."

"Well, greetings, Miriam. You are just a slip of a girl, but I think you will do just fine. There is plenty to keep a household servant busy. You will never be bored." The mistress turned towards her husband, and said with a purr, "So, I see you received my message, Naaman. You did well in choosing a maid."

"To tell you the truth, I had little to do with it, Adara. I left it up to Galius. He found her running across his path as our soldiers passed through Shunem town. She has some spunk, I'm told. And, I can see a touch of it now." He studied Miriam's face, and, as he did, she raised her chin in defiance, then set her jaw and turned away, hoping her slowly reddening face wouldn't betray her feelings.

Passed through the town. Indeed. How about scouring, scourging or ransacking? Those are better words. Miriam held her breath, trying to control the rage building inside. Her body began to tremble. *Control your feelings, Miriam. You'll never get back home if you show anger.*

CHAPTER SIX

ADARA LOOKED UP, SHIFTING FORWARD in her lounging couch and gave him a quick, non-committal smile.

"And, what of her family? What happened to her father and mother?" the mistress asked.

The question took Miriam by surprise. She straightened, her hopes rising along with her spirits. With all her heart and soul, she wished—

"Galius did not mention her family. I don't know." The commander seemed matter of fact, shaking his head.

Doesn't know? He means he doesn't care. How arrogant. How—The bitterness returned, and Miriam found it difficult to squelch it this time. She stiffened, pressing her lips together.

The mistress noticed, and quickly addressed her husband. "Naaman, we mustn't talk about it now. It seems to have troubled the girl."

He shrugged his muscular shoulders, oblivious of the grief it was causing. Smiling briefly at his wife, the master said, "I will leave the girl to you, my dear. Train her as you wish."

He turned and left the room, his heavy steps echoing in the stone hallway.

They also echoed through Miriam's heart, which grew hard, cold, and empty, too. *What is the use of living if all those I love are gone?*

After her husband took his leave, Adara nodded towards Miriam, then noticed Vashti waiting at the entrance of the room.

"Come in, Vashti, dear. Meet my new servant girl."

The girl obeyed, her cheeks reddening as she made her way across the room. For a moment, Miriam was distracted with her dress, a flowing thin fabric gathered at the waist with a gold cord, which swayed with her forward movement. *She has the appearance of a princess,* Miriam thought.

Miriam intently examined a crack in the floor, not sure what would happen next.

"Vashti, this is Miriam. She is a long way from home. Be kind. And, although it is not proper for you to befriend her, she needs compassion." Adara's tender voice drew Miriam's gaze upward. As Miriam looked into the soft, gentle eyes of her new mistress, tears began to well.

"This must be difficult for you, Miriam. War is never easy. Leaving the ones you love is never easy."

Miriam's tears began to fall. She couldn't help herself. She felt weak and vulnerable. Her fists clenched, as she prepared to speak.

"It didn't have to be this way! Your people didn't need to invade our tiny village. What does it matter?" She immediately regretted her bitter speech.

"Come, my little one. I may not be your mother, but I have comforted a child in distress. Let me try to soothe your pain."

Miriam immediately had two desires fighting within her heart. One was to run towards the mistress and get lost in her embrace, like she would have with her ima. How she longed for her comforting embrace. But *not* from the enemy.

The other was to run down the hall and out the door towards freedom. To run anywhere. But what good would that accomplish? It couldn't bring her family back.

Ultimately, she chose a third. Slowly Miriam looked up and stared into those uncommonly green eyes as she crossed her arms tightly in front of her body. *No one will get close to me. I won't give my heart away to be broken. Not to someone whose husband destroyed my family.* She stood her ground, holding on tightly to all that was familiar. Holding on to the past—and to hope itself.

CHAPTER SEVEN

"IT'S ALL RIGHT, MY DEAR. For now. But you must learn to obey. I will need to trust you, Miriam. I need a trustworthy servant."

Miriam looked away, mixed emotions tugging at her. Just then, she caught sight of another person in the room, a servant girl, about her age, watching Miriam intently from the doorway. Her eyes looked troubled. In fact, she looked almost angry.

Mistress Adara glanced in the direction of Miriam's stare. "Rana, come here. Meet Miriam, our new servant, and my personal assistant."

The girl's eyes flashed anger this time, jaw clenched as she hesitated.

"Rana, come." The girl remained in her place. "Come, I said." The mistress spoke more strongly this time, then addressed Vashti standing in the entrance of the courtyard looking on. "Dear, get your things ready for your trip to your cousin's. You will leave with Ahmad at sunrise. The heat is too oppressive for travel later in the day, you know that."

Vashti bowed slightly. "Yes, mother. And—" she turned towards Miriam, "I'm glad you are here." Miriam turned to the girl, then drew in a breath. *She has her mother's eyes!* Barely able to tear her gaze away, she watched a tiny grin forming on Vashti's captivating face. Miriam returned the smile, drawn to her gentle spirit. With a twirl and a light step, Vashti went to do her mother's bidding.

Rana grimaced at Vashti as she passed, then turned towards Miriam, glaring up and down at her disapprovingly, her sly smile mocking the newcomer in silence.

What an unhappy girl. Do I look that way to others?

"Miriam will be taking your place, Rana," said Adara. "You know we have talked about this. Your meddling and unkind ways are the reason for the change. She will need your assistance in the next few days as she learns her duties. I ask you to be efficient in this, Rana. Be thankful we are not turning you out. You will, of course, be helping with the other household chores on a daily basis."

Rana bowed her head quickly, giving the mistress a swift and shallow curtsy. *This will be a challenge, I'm sure,* Miriam pondered. *I wonder what stories she has to tell?*

"You may now return to your duties, Rana. And call Jamal. I need to speak to him as well."

Without looking up, the servant girl replied, "Yes, mistress," bowed slightly and left the room.

"That girl is indeed stubborn. But, she has learned some good skills, and can teach you much." Adara raised her index finger warningly. "But, beware. Don't let her lead you astray."

Miriam locked eyes with her mistress for a few seconds, then nodded her head politely.

"Jamal," Adara called. A young man came in through the doorway. He was taller than Miriam, and thinner. A brown cloth was wrapped around his head, making his big, brown eyes even more pronounced. His skin blended with his simple light brown tunic clinched around his waist with a rope.

"Yes, mistress?" His voice was a bit raspy, as if he had just awakened from a nap.

"Take Miriam to her lodging and introduce her to the remainder of the staff."

"Certainly, mistress," he said with a broad smile. His bright white teeth stood in contrast to his sun-tanned face. He motioned for Miriam to follow him.

The remainder of the evening was a blur. Jamal took her on a tour of the courtyard and living quarters of the staff, as well as the common areas the servants were allowed freely to roam as they performed their duties. He introduced her to the rotund cook, who was making goat's cheese for the next morning's meal.

"Well, hello, young miss! Welcome to our humble kitchen. I'm Phoebe, the cook." Her voice was laced with laughter as she spoke.

Next, she met the commander's tall and rather robust manservant and the sheepish stable boy, who seemed both shy and mute. He only nodded in greeting. They passed by Rana who, as Jamal explained, was now responsible for washing the entire staff and master's clothes and dishes and performing the necessary odd jobs. Each time Miriam looked her way, the girl turned her head away.

Then, Miriam's worst fear was realized when Jamal brought her to her lodgings; a tiny room with a high, small window at the back of the sunbaked home. There were two cots squeezed in. One was disheveled and obviously in use. The other, neatly made. *No, it can't be. I can't be boarding with—with—her?*

CHAPTER EIGHT

"MIRIAM—THIS IS YOUR BED. YOU will be sharing the room with Rana. The housekeeper requests that you keep your bed made, and the room clean at all times," said Jamal.

She looked around the sparsely furnished room. *Now I'm truly a captive. This will be my prison.* Her eye caught a small stone image on the windowsill above her head—a figure whose head was an orb with jagged rays shooting from it. Miriam heard her parents talking about the gods of heathen nations.

"Is-is that an idol?" she asked Jamal timidly.

"It is our main god, Rimmon—the sun god. It brings us luck. And a bountiful harvest."

"What do you mean—luck?" Miriam's brow furrowed.

"Good fortune. Favor. Helps us be strong and brave. Don't you believe in luck?"

Miriam looked down at her dusty sandals. "No."

Jamal seemed puzzled. "What do you believe in then?"

Miriam wasn't sure she was ready to reveal her faith. Truly, did she really have one? Or, did it belong to her parents? She wasn't sure if she believed anymore in a Jehovah who would allow her family and village to be destroyed.

"Nothing? You believe in nothing?" Jamal's mouth hung open.

Now she felt the need to defend herself. "I believe in our Father Abraham. In the all-powerful, mighty Jehovah."

There. She said it. Somehow, she felt like a liar. *Do I really mean those words?*

The young servant's eyes widened, raising one eyebrow. He seemed to gather thoughts through them.

"Do you mean the God who parted the sea? And blew down the walls of Jericho?"

Miriam startled at his comment, blinked in amazement. "Yes—Exactly."

"We have heard the reports," Jamal said, "from many merchants who travel through our land. A miracle-making God, they say."

Miriam revealed a tiny smile. To think there might be someone on her side. A flicker of hope rose in her heart. Someone who wouldn't make fun of her people and their strange ways.

The two stood silently for a moment, examining each other in a curious manner. *He is the big brother I never had—he could be a friend in this strange place.* Jamal shifted his feet and took a deep breath.

"Well—I must be about my master's business. Is there anything you need before I go?" Jamal's tone turned impersonal.

"No. Not at all. Thank you."

Jamal bowed ever so slightly, and then exited quickly.

Now alone, Miriam climbed onto the lumpy bed padded with straw. Her eyes wandered once more to the high windowsill. She carefully stood on the edge of the bed and reached up to touch the small figure standing still and straight. *Thou shalt have no other gods before me.* The commandment repeated itself in her mind. But what other gods are there? *Will You forsake me in this strange new land? Will I forsake You?*

Suddenly, her foot slipped, knocking herself and the idol to the floor with a crash. Miriam's eyes squeezed shut listening to the swift footsteps heading her way. She held her breath, hoping it wasn't—

Rana burst into the room, but stopped short, staring down in horror at the broken image on the unforgiving stone floor.

CHAPTER NINE

"WHAT HAVE YOU DONE?" HER eyes blazed with fire. "How could you? It was NOT yours to touch. Now we are both in trouble with the gods."

Miriam attempted to pull herself off the cold surface, and up onto her knees. "I am sorry. Truly sorry. I did not mean to break it. I was curious."

"Ha! Doesn't your God forbid other gods? Isn't He jealous? Now you are twice in trouble."

Miriam wondered how she knew so much about the Hebrew's Jehovah.

"Last year we had an Israelite slave boy to serve the master. He didn't last long." Rana sneered. "But we got an earful of your strange ways before he departed. And you? How long will you stay? A week? A month?" She derided. "We will see what we can do about that."

"I will fix it. I will try." Miriam reached for the jagged pieces.

"Don't touch it. Don't you dare." Rana pointed a long, slender finger at Miriam. "I don't want your filthy Hebrew hands touching my god."

No more words were needed. Miriam flung herself on her bed, with her face to the wall. She listened as Rana hurriedly picked up all the pieces, and stomped out of the room, talking under her breath in harsh tones. A tear found its way through Miriam's eyelids, squeezed shut from grief. What she wouldn't give for a hug from her ima, or a pat on the shoulders from abba. *Is there no one to love me?* Exhausted with these thoughts, she fell fast asleep.

Miriam awoke with a start. Did someone slap her foot?

"Get up, you lazy girl! Get up this instant, or I will report you to the mistress." The thorny words made her wince.

It was Rana. *Did I sleep that long? Is it truly morning?* She turned towards the ever-present blinding sun streaming into the small raised window. She instantly shielded her eyes. Yes. It was true. *What a way to start the day.* Rana was as mean as ever.

Miriam set her jaw and shot her a stern look, lips stretching into a thin line. Then she rose, straightened her disheveled, dark and matted hair, quickly dressed in her wrinkled garb and headed towards the kitchen.

"Girl, I was wondering what happened to you." Phoebe, the cook, was preparing flatbread on a stone over the fire. "We must hurry with the morning meal. The master is leaving early for town today and must be fed. Come now!"

"Yes, ma'am." Miriam bowed slightly, then turned to look at Rana, waiting for instruction.

It was odd to accept help from someone she was meant to be in charge of. But Rana just stared at Miriam, standing lifeless like a pillar. Then she raised her eyebrows in expectation. Miriam's temper was rising, but she tried not to let it show. Taking a deep breath, she asked, to no one in particular:

"What needs to be done first?"

Miriam waited, hands folded patiently. It seemed an eternity before Phoebe spoke.

"Done first? I need to explain your duties, too?" The once jovial voice became vexed.

Rana snickered—but not for long. Phoebe took notice, and placing one hand on her hip, and with the other became animated, shaking her finger at the unruly servant girl.

"What did the mistress tell you, Rana? You *must* teach this young girl your job. It wasn't my fault that you lost your position. Teach her what she needs to know. Quickly!" The cook dismissed them with a sweeping hand.

Begrudgingly, the pouting servant girl began the task of orienting Miriam to her responsibilities. She showed her which pottery to use, how to serve the master and mistress, and when to clear the plates. Rana also mentioned a list of their favorite foods, and another list of mannerisms that annoyed them.

"The mistress likes her dish served from the left side. And she always leaves a bit of food on her plate, and wants it removed at once."

The girl spoke in hushed tones, which Miriam thought odd. Rana went on and on and on. Miriam wasn't sure she could remember all the rules. Her head was reeling with information.

I must do my best. Maybe then, after a few months of good behavior, they will let me go back home. She was hopeful, anyway.

CHAPTER TEN

A FEW DAYS LATER, THE commander returned. The staff hurried to prepare for the celebration. The master and mistress reclined at a low wood table, plucking grapes from their stems and popping them in their mouths as they awaited the meal. Adara sat up, glancing towards the opening to the dining area. A relieved sigh escaped her as Rana and Miriam marched in with plates of olives and pickled eggplant, fried salted goat cheese and Falafel balls made with chickpeas, and a small dish of fresh tomatoes and cucumber topped with mint leaves. Adara's eyes were all aglow as she witnessed the procession.

"Delightful! My favorite foods. And the timing is perfect. Somehow, today, I am extremely hungry. It seems days since I've had the appetite to enjoy a hearty meal with the master gone." Adara inhaled the aroma surrounding her as the girls began to serve the meal.

"Delicious. It smells delicious. I hope I'm not disappointed. Let's see. Is it my favorite, lamb and onion stew?"

Miriam curtsied, and began to say, "Yes, Mistress. It is . . . " But Rana broke in.

"No. Even better. It's Mahshi, zucchini stuffed with minced lamb and rice. I suggested it to the cook, Mistress. I thought you might like it for the master's homecoming." Her face burst into a prideful smile. Miriam's eyebrows lifted. She didn't like the untruth being spoken. So, that was Rana's game, was it?

Miriam carefully placed the Mahshi onto two clay dishes, filling the master's with twice as much. She put the pot down off to the side, preparing to serve them. *He must be hungry, too.* Although she wondered why she would bother to bless a man who destroyed her village. Maybe she should serve him less. It's what he deserved.

Rana immediately picked up the full dish and presented it to the master.

"You must be hungry after your conquest, Master. Here is a bit extra for you." She smiled slyly.

Miriam bit her lip. She was close to bursting out the truth in anger but held back. Picking up the smaller portion, she served it from the left, as Rana had taught her.

"NOT on my left, girl! On my right. Have you not listened to Rana's instructions?" Adara's brow was furrowed and her voice, sharp. It was so unlike the mistress that it startled Miriam. She dropped a serving spoon on the tile floor, wincing as it banged and clattered on the stone surface. Her face turned red with embarrassment, and then aggravation and finally, confusion.

"I—she—Rana . . ."

Miriam glanced at Rana who shot daggers at her, eyes squinting their threats in response.

"Yes, ma'am. I'm sorry. I will remember next time. Serve on the right." Miriam bowed slightly and retrieved the utensil from the floor.

"I'll clean up the mess, Mistress."

"Good. And we won't need to mention it again, will we?" The mistress sounded gentler now.

"No. You won't, Mistress. Sorry." Miriam's head was bowed, her eyes fixed on the spoon in her shaking hand. She wanted to run from the room and hide in the stables.

Instead, after her duties were done, with barely a word to anyone, and without taking food or drink herself, Miriam ran to the roof of the house. There, she could think and pray amongst the drying herbs and spices. The bubbling sound of falling water from the fountain in the courtyard echoed against the stone walls, soothing her troubled soul.

She laid her head on her arm, tears trailing down her cheek. Thoughts of home flooded her mind. Her heart was back in Israel where the grapes and pomegranates were sweet, and the barley filled the hungry with bread. Miriam's countenance turned as sour as her spirits. Her empty stomach growled as she thought of her friends.

"Just a month ago, we were laughing and playing with no thought of tomorrow. I want to go back. I can't stand it here anymore," she said to the emptiness.

Freely, her thoughts flowed as the streams running through her homeland. One part of her wanted to push Rana to the dusty ground. She wanted to turn the bears on her enemy like the prophet Elisha when the boys mocked him.

The other part of her, the part that held the holy writ inside, chose to be silent. To take the persecution with no thought of fighting back. *Always do what is good and right, Miriam,* she could hear her mother say. *Leave no room for the devil to bury in your heart.*

Miriam began to weep loudly, unable to hold back her tears. Her shoulders quaked as she took in large gasps of air, her breath catching with each attempt. She couldn't keep up this charade. She had made her decision.

Oh, Abba Father! I am so sorry. I have grieved You—the very one who has loved me all my life. Watched over me with care. Given me what was best. Father, remove my stubborn heart. Replace it with a soft and sensitive spirit.

She, with Jehovah's help, would be good and kind. She would take whatever Rana would give her. She would be the best lady's maid ever, to honor Jehovah and her parents. Most importantly, Jehovah. Whether her parents were still alive or not, she did not know. But no matter what the future held, she, Miriam, child of the Most High, would be faithful.

CHAPTER ELEVEN

THAT EVENING, THE MISTRESS CALLED for Miriam. Her flowing dark hair needed to be brushed. It soothed Miriam's spirits to unwind the jeweled cords wound around her braid. She took a slow deep breath as she loosened the hair and began massaging Adara's scalp with the fragrant oil of sandalwood. Miriam let out a sigh, then continued, running her fingers along the length of the mistress's tresses, kneading the oils into the thick strands. The demands of the day seemed to melt away as she closed her eyes and thought again of home.

"Miriam?"

The sound of her name shook her to attention. As she opened her eyes, Miriam found herself looking straight into a reflection of Mistress Adara, who was holding a mirror to her face. The corners of the mistress's mouth turned gently upward.

"Yes, Mistress?"

"Were you told to serve me on my left?"

"Yes, Mistress."

She frowned and continued. "I thought as much. Rana is not happy with her new position. Of course, she would take it out on you. I will speak to her."

"Thank you, Mistress." Miriam relaxed her shoulders, not realizing they were tensed.

"Remember—I must be able to trust you. Understood? Now, Miriam, would you light the oil lamp for our god, Rimmon? He has brought my husband home to me, and I am grateful."

Miriam was unsure of what to do. And how to do it. Most importantly, should she do it? What would Elisha the prophet think? Disobey the Almighty who demanded righteousness and obey her mistress? Or obey Jehovah and risk punishment? She stood still as a stone.

"Miriam? Did you hear my request?"

"Yes, Mistress, I did."

"Well, then, go on. Do as I said."

"But I . . . I don't . . . I can't . . . " Miriam shook her head, her body tensing again, all the calm gone. Tears welled up against her silent command.

"Oh, I see. Of course. No other gods. The Hebrew motto."

"Yes, Mistress. I don't want to disobey the Almighty. But—" she added immediately, "I also don't want to disobey you."

"Ah, I see your problem. I'm not asking you to worship Rimmon. I'm only asking you to light the lamp."

Is it really that important? I'm not worshiping the god. Just lighting the lamp.

These thoughts swirled in her head as she mechanically did as she was told. As the oiled wick caught the flame and began to burn, she thought of the wrath of the all-powerful Jehovah poured out on the prophets of Baal. *Am I as bad as they?*

Miriam finished her task, bowed quickly to Mistress Adara, then hastened to her room. The oil lamp had already gone out. Rana was sound asleep, her heavy breathing echoing off the stone walls. Miriam tiptoed to her bed, feeling for the frame. She undressed and lay down, her heart and head heavy as the night, thoughts invading her sleep like enemy soldiers.

The next afternoon, all seemed bright again. Miriam attended to her mistress as Adara sat at her loom. Brilliant red, purple, and blue threads intermingled with bronze graced the tapestry, now a hand span in length. Miriam's eyes were fixed on the shuttle as she cooled her mistress with a palm leaf. The day was especially hot. They could all feel the oppressive heat, which put the entire household out of sorts.

"Miriam, tell me more stories of your people. A people with a nation, and—so I've heard—a strong faith. I have need for a diversion to keep my mind off this hot spell."

"Yes, Mistress," she said, her eyes widening. *Does my mistress truly desire to know about our faith?*

Miriam crinkled her forehead, pondering the possibilities. There was so much she could say. So many people she could speak about. Then finally, it came to her.

"Joseph was a Hebrew who was despised by his brothers. They were jealous because his father, Jacob, seemed to love him best. He had a coat of many colors, much like your cloth here on the loom, that he made especially for his son. Joseph was the beloved of Jacob's favorite wife, Rachel. But she died laboring at the birth of his brother a few years later. The father was bereaved, so he placed his love on the shoulders of Joseph, making his ten older brothers angry. So angry, in fact, that they sold him as a slave one day to a caravan passing through their town."

"How that father must have grieved," said Adara, shaking her head, her fingers deftly working the loom.

"Yes, but it was much worse. The brothers lied and said he was killed by a wild beast to cover up their sin. They even smeared animal blood on Joseph's beautiful coat and brought it to their father to prove he had met his fate on the road." Miriam stopped fanning, so intent was she on telling her story. The mistress barely noticed.

"Oh, my! How could he bear it?"

"For years Jacob assumed his son was dead. He grieved for him every day."

"And then? What happened to this treasured son—this Joseph?"

"He was sold as a slave to Potiphar in Egypt. Potiphar was a very influential man. Joseph was such a good worker that his master's house was blessed because of him. But, one day, Potiphar's wife accused Joseph of attacking her, which was false. But, he was put in jail nonetheless."

"How unfair!" The mistress cried, raising her hands in alarm. Turning to Miriam, she motioned for her to resume fanning. Then, Miriam continued her story, deep in thought.

"True. Nevertheless, our Almighty Yahweh gave Joseph a gift. He could interpret dreams. One day, Jehovah sent a disturbing dream to Pharaoh. And the only one able to interpret it was Joseph. The ruler's dream was about the years of abundance followed by years of famine that were coming to Egypt."

"So? And then?" The mistress sat up, hanging on Miriam's every word.

"Miraculously, Pharaoh, seeing his gift, put Joseph in charge of gathering grain during the seven abundant years, so they could sell it to the people of the land in the seven lean years. Joseph saved not only the Egyptians, but his own family as well. But, that's another story."

"Your God brought Joseph to Egypt at just the right time it seems," Adara said with a sideways glance and with it came a sweet smile.

"Yes, He did. For such a time as this. Joseph had to be taken from his family and endure many hardships to do Jehovah's will and save many."

"Hmmmm." The mistress seemed deep in thought as she stared at her weaving. "So, if I could hold this cloth above my head, these tangled threads on the underside are like the trials in our lives. They make no sense—all is confusion. But your God above sees a beautiful pattern on the topside. He sees how everything that happens in your lives comes together in a wonderful and meaningful way. Although you were snatched from your home in what seems to be a senseless act, maybe you were brought to our home, Miriam, for a special purpose."

"Maybe." Miriam grinned. She was beginning to like her mistress. To like her very well.

Out of the corner of her eye, Miriam noticed Rana hiding near the archway behind a palm tree. Her scowl said it all. Miriam's pleasant feeling vanished. *What will she try to do to me now?*

"May I go, Mistress?" asked Miriam, eyes darting from Adara to Rana then back again.

"Of course. You can tell me more tomorrow." Adara's eyes gleamed.

"I would be honored, my lady."

She bowed slightly and made a move towards Rana, but the girl quickly scooted from the room. Miriam followed her towards the kitchen where she found the servant girl busying herself cutting mint leaves for the evening meal.

"Did you want to speak to me, Rana?" Miriam decided it was time to be kind. Rana stopped her knife mid-air and glared at her competitor.

"Why would I want to talk to you? You deceitful little thing. Trying to get in good with the mistress and making trouble for me."

"Not at all Rana. Why can't you believe me?"

"You were sent by the gods to heckle me. So, I must fight."

"Fight me, or the gods?" Miriam laughed inwardly at that one.

"Fight you, of course. One can't bear arms against a god."

Now was her chance.

"That is true, Rana. I have shaken my fists at my Jehovah, but I get nowhere. I don't know why He puts up with me sometimes." She shrugged.

Rana looked intently at Miriam, frowning.

"You talk as if He was a friend of yours. How can a god be a friend? Impossible! They are cunning and cruel, and delight to make mischief in our days, so we spend our lives burning incense to please them." Rana began cutting herbs again, this time, with quick and forceful movements.

"The only way I can please the Almighty One is to obey Him. Our King David said He wants obedience rather than sacrifice."

"But how can you know what He wants? Our gods are made of stone and wood and can't hear or see. Although sometimes we act like they can."

"We can know about Him from reading the Torah. It's filled with words straight from the mouth of Yahweh. And sometimes, the words come to us from the prophets, like Elisha."

"Girls. Girls!" A voice cut into their conversation.

"There is much to be done. It's time to sweep the floor and trim the lamps for the evening meal. No time for talking."

It was Phoebe again. She seemed to be in charge of everything, not only the kitchen. She seemed to have lost her jovial spirit, now that the master was home. All was work and no play to her. Rana and Miriam obeyed, this time agreeably, locking eyes for an instant with a quick nod, raised eyebrows and a tiny smile. Finally—an obstacle they could tackle together.

At the end of the evening, they were exhausted. They fell into bed, the cool stone walls of their inner room a welcome relief from the blistering day. And for the first time, there was no tension between them. They were fast asleep within minutes.

CHAPTER TWELVE

NEXT MORNING, AS RANA AND Miriam went to ask the master and mistress what they would like for their morning meal, they chatted like fast friends along the way. As the girls headed down the passageway, they overheard heated words echoing off the unforgiving walls in the master's private room.

"My dear, don't take just one doctor's diagnosis. It could be nothing. Or something other than that . . . that . . . dreaded disease."

"Say it, Adara. Say it! LEPROSY. I'll never fight in another war. Never again be a commander for the king's army. Never vanquish another foe. What good am I?"

"Naaman. Please." The girls had never heard their mistress call her husband by his familiar name.

"Let's find another opinion. There are many reputable doctors in Syria. And we haven't sacrificed to the gods yet. That simple act could be our salvation."

"I don't want the entire world to know, Adara. These things must be kept to ourselves until we know for sure."

"So, you *don't* believe it's leprosy, do you my dear? Oh, I'm so glad." Adara's voice softened with hope.

A metal object thrown inside the master's bedroom, landed with an awful clatter. Listening outside the door, the girls looked at each other with amazement and a touch of fear.

"I don't know anything for sure anymore!" The commander's voice broke.

"Dear, sit down. Let's think about this. Think about who can help us. And someone, of course, who can keep a secret. Come here. Sit against this pillow and relax. What you need right now is a flask of wine," the mistress said with a soothing tone. "Rana! Miriam? Come now." Her voice became immediately insistent.

The two servant girls glanced at one another, ashamed at eavesdropping. They answered in unison, "Yes, mistress?" Then they tiptoed to the doorway and peeked in.

"Oh. There you are. Get the master a flask of wine—and bitter herbs. He is in need of them directly. And bring some fresh grapes and dates."

"Yes, mistress!" they said with one voice, bowing.

The girls found a flask with the cook's help, put some bitter herbs in a tiny bowl, and arranged the requested fruit in a decorative manner in a clay bowl. *I hope the master will be pleased and forget about his ailment.* Miriam surprised herself. Who would have guessed that in such a short time, she would be wishing peace to the man who destroyed her village and family? That *was* a miracle.

Miriam and Rana brought in the tray and flask of wine quietly, not wanting to irritate the situation even more. As Miriam drew closer to pour the drink, she noticed a discolored patch of whitened skin on the back of her master's hand, now partially covering his forehead and eyes.

"Thank you, girls," the mistress said, looking up at Miriam, who thought her eyes seemed worried and sad.

The two servants bowed slightly, backed out of the room and returned to the kitchen. *Only a miracle can help the master now.* Miriam's eyes moistened. Was that compassion she was feeling?

All day, as Miriam went about her duties, she kept thinking of the master and his ailment. She didn't remember any friends or family with leprosy. But, she had heard of the terrible effects: disfigured faces, distorted limbs and rotting flesh peeling away like grape skins. Cries of "Unclean! Unclean!" from their hopeless faces, forced them to push away beloved friends and family. She couldn't imagine, conqueror or not, her master being plagued with the disease.

What did her people do in times of despair or sickness? Of course, they prayed. And offered sacrifices just in case it was caused by their sin. Sometimes, they would use a potion that a Levite priest would prescribe. Usually, it was an herb. *But which one would they use for sores?* Miriam pondered some more.

CHAPTER THIRTEEN

LATER IN THE AFTERNOON, MISTRESS Adara was resting in the shade of a palm tree in the courtyard. She was gazing into the distance, unaware of Miriam's approach.

"Mistress?" Miriam spoke louder than normal to be heard over the sound of the flowing fountain.

Adara shook herself back to reality. "Yes, Miriam, what is it?"

"Sorry to disturb your rest. I hope I'm not bringing offense, mistress, but, I overheard your conversation with the master. And I'd like to help if I could."

"Well, that is kind of you, Miriam. But I'm sure there is nothing a young girl like you can do to remedy the situation." The mistress shook her head, sighed, then rested it in her upturned hands.

"Please listen, Mistress—back in my hometown in Samaria, we treat skin sores with the oleander plant. My mother would gather them from the roadside, crush the roots and bark with a mortar and pestle, lay it on the sore, wrap a leaf over it, and tie it with a cord. I've also heard those from wealthy households used saffron to prevent the plague. Perhaps it might help the master?"

"I have used saffron. But oleander? I am not familiar with that remedy. I would suppose our priests would know of it. I will send Jamal to the temple today. Thank you, Miriam."

"You are welcome my lady." Miriam turned and began walking away but halted when her mistress continued to speak.

"I know it hasn't been easy for you here in a strange land. And I'm sure you do not like the master for what he has done to your village and people. So, I am grateful for your help and your concern. Is there something I can do for you?"

"Going home to my family is all I think about. It's all I care about," said Miriam, eyes pleading.

"Well, I'm afraid that is the one thing I *can't* help you with. There is no way to find your family, Miriam. You will need to be content with your life here in Syria."

A familiar bitterness began to erupt slowly inside. Miriam's heart pounded, her face turning red. Clenching her fists, she let it burst forth without a fight.

"I can't! I just can't. I've *got* to go home. Ima *needs* me. I *know* she does!"

Miriam broke down in sobs, kneeling on the hard ground, her forehead touching its cool surface. Somehow, it was comforting. Almost like a cool rag ima would rest on her forehead when she was sick. Miriam felt a hand gently touch her back. She jerked her body instantly away, then regretted her action. Hadn't she settled this once and for all?

The mistress stood up quietly and walked out of the room, leaving Miriam to wallow in self-pity.

How—oh how can I be brave? What if—

She spoke out loud, to an empty room: "I don't care if the master dies of the disease. He deserves it! For all he has done to my people. And my family most of all."

Shocked and ashamed at her outburst and hateful words, she ran—as fast as her sandaled feet would carry her—through the sheltered courtyard and out into the expansive vineyard. The sun was setting, coloring the greening hills a gentle orange. Row after row of grapevines hung on latticed framework, heavy with ripening fruit. Turning into the first row, she continued her run down its length until she tripped and fell from exhaustion. Still on her knees, resting her forehead on the ground, hands shielding her swollen eyes, she began to weep. Bitterness and sorrow flowing together as the tears spilled to the ground.

CHAPTER FOURTEEN

SHE LAMENTED—HER SPIRIT BREAKING. FOR her parents. For her brother. For her village. And, for her hardened heart. She was so ashamed. How could she face Adara again? Would she ever gain victory and trust in Jehovah?

Abba Father, help me to forgive. Melt my heart. Take my stubborn will and replace it with a moldable one. I want to be clay in the potter's hands— Your hands, Abba. You know what is best.

She raised her head momentarily, wiping her tear-stained face with her sleeve. Just then, her eyes were drawn to a movement at the end of the row. A man in shaggy clothes and a red turban tried to hide himself by creeping sideways, pressing against the abundance of large green leaves along the vines. She could see him, but he did not notice her presence. Miriam could tell he was not one of the servants; none of them dressed in such a strange manner. When he crawled under the lattice and into the next column of vines, she made a note to tell Adara what she saw, then turned her attention inward once again to grieve.

Miriam thought of her loving ima who never hurt anyone. She tried only to help—even those who wronged her. Like the woman in the village who said her mother gave her the wrong remedy for a stomach ache. Said she retched all day.

Ima was never wrong with her remedies. But she took the criticism without lashing back. The woman never spoke to her again. Then neighbors began to avoid her, afraid to ask help for what ailed them.

"How could my mother be so patient and loving?" Miriam questioned herself. She allowed her head to fall against the latticework and then closed her eyes. Another tear trailed down her smudged cheek.

"Ima, what would you do if you were me? Help this man who destroyed our family?" Miriam asked the clouds.

Never repay evil for evil . . . only good, Miriam. She could hear her mother saying these exact words.

"I'm trying, Ima. Really, I am! But it's just so *hard*."

Miriam laid her body on the cool dry ground under the shelter of the vines and fell fast asleep. Dreams flitted through with images of her family, her village, and, strangely, of the prophet Elisha who lived in town with a widow and her son. She saw that widow's son raised from the dead, witnessing the joy bursting over the mother's face when he took a life-giving breath.

Miriam awakened with a start when she heard her name being called from a distance. How long had she been asleep? She pushed herself up from the ground and began her trek towards the house. As she passed by a tamarisk tree full of white blossoms, her toe kicked something near its base, propelling it forward.

What is this? She picked up a leather pouch which had been hastily tied with a thin rope. *Hmmmmm.*

She unfolded the pouch and pulled out the contents. Miriam's eyes became round in wonderment. *A jeweled idol. Made of gold!* Then she remembered the man fleeing among the grapevines. *A thief.*

Her mother's words played in her mind once again. *Never repay evil for evil.* Miriam now knew exactly what she should do.

CHAPTER FIFTEEN

"MIRIAM. *MIRIAM!*" IT WAS JAMAL, urging her forward with his waving hand.

"We've been looking for you. The mistress was worried. Come. Come back to the house."

Miriam was reluctant but obeyed, hiding the pouch between the folds of her skirt. Coming alongside Jamal she met his stride.

"My dear, are you well?" The mistress beckoned her towards the cushion on the ground where she was seated. "Come—sit, Miriam."

Still drowsy from her nap in the vineyard, Miriam shuffled towards her and sank into the other pillow positioned beside her mistress: her hand still clutching her skirt for fear the pouch would slip out.

"Miriam, I am sorry for taking your hope away. I have been concerned with my husband's condition and did not consider your feelings at all. Let's be friends—if that is possible."

She looked down at the girl, waiting for an answer.

Miriam softened. Seeing compassion in her mistress's eyes, she gave Adara what she wanted. A small smile crept across her face.

"That's better. Now go and help Rana gather herbs drying on the roof. Phoebe needs them to prepare our evening meal. You must be hungry, too. Ask her to break off a piece of barley loaf for you."

"Yes, mistress."

Miriam got up to leave, still clutching her skirt.

"My dear, what is it? What do you have hidden there?"

Miriam slowly brought out the pouch. The mistress's eyes furrowed. "What is it?"

"It-it's something that belongs to you, I think."

"To me?" The mistress pointed to herself, still puzzled.

"Yes. When I was—when I ran out to the vineyard, I saw a man in ragged clothes and a red turban running down the rows. I must have frightened him. But I thought nothing of it and fell off to sleep. When I awoke, I found this bag beneath the grass on my way back to the house. When I looked inside, I found—" Miriam held out the pouch. "This."

The mistress opened the pouch and peeked in with amazement. "My precious idol! What—How?"

"I believe it was a thief, mistress. When you were having the talk with the master, he must have come in to steal it."

"And you must have frightened him away, Miriam. Someone has been stealing food from the kitchen these last few days. And now, *this*. It's true! You have come to us to help us. We thank you, Miriam. No—*I* thank you. And now, I can fully trust you. You could have kept the idol in spite. Or somehow run away and sold it. Come, Miriam. I'm so proud of you!"

The mistress opened her arms to hug her. This time, Miriam ran into them. And wept.

Adara stroked Miriam's long brown tresses. After a while, she spoke. "Go, Miriam. Ask Phoebe for that barley loaf. You certainly have earned it." The mistress patted Miriam's head and released her.

Back in the kitchen she heartily partook of the welcomed snack. The bread soothed Miriam's spirits, allowing her to continue her daily chores. Nightfall came before she knew it. The hooting owls put her gently at peace as the cool night wrapped her in its blanket. She soon drifted off to sleep, her cares left for another day.

CHAPTER SIXTEEN

THE DAYS MOVED SWIFTLY BY as Miriam learned to work and live in the master's household.

A week later, just rising from a pleasant night's sleep, she heard muffled conversation and, at times, raised, high-pitched voices echoing from the courtyard. Miriam washed her face in a bowl of water, put on her brown tunic, and wrapped a piece of multicolored fabric around her waist. She slipped her leather sandals on her tanned feet and made her way to the cook's quarters. Mumbling voices became clearer and louder as she walked down the hall. What she heard made her hesitate.

"They have confirmed it, Adara. It is leprosy. I am finished. There is no denying the cause of these white patches appearing on my body."

"But, my dear, have we truly tried everything? Contacting physicians, sacrificing to the gods, trying magician's remedies?"

"Yes . . . all but sacrificing a sacred thing. Something special we love."

"Oh, no, Naaman. You can't mean it. We cannot . . . our precious daughter?"

Miriam let out a small cry, but immediately covered her mouth. *Vashti? They want to sacrifice Vashti? Oh, Protector of our Fathers . . . no! Please don't let this happen.*

This beautiful young girl, away for a few weeks with a cousin, won Miriam's heart almost immediately the first and only time they met—with her doe-like eyes and graceful movements. In her mind, Miriam saw this gentle girl, with skin as bronze as the barley fields at harvest, lying bound on a pile of wood. The master's voice brought her to attention:

"We have given our cattle and sheep and goats. There is one more sacrifice we can make. One much dearer!"

"No. I will not hear of it. How could you, Naaman? Is your health worth the sacrifice? Is it?"

Adara burst into tears and fled from the room, her long flowing gown billowing in the breeze, not noticing Miriam as she passed.

Miriam recalled the holy man Elijah battling the prophets of Baal. *Choose you this day whom you will serve. The prophets tried and failed to get an answer from their god. My master will never get an answer. But that's not the worst of it.* Miriam considered. *Vashti will be DEAD. She will be sacrificed for nothing! But what can I do? I am just a young girl.*

Thoughts of Elijah and his power from the Most High made Miriam pause. *He is no longer on this earth. But what about Elisha? He healed the widow's son and provided flour and oil until the famine was over. Could he—would he—know what to do?*

That afternoon, Miriam crept over to Adara as she worked at her loom, reluctant to disturb her mistress. Looking over her shoulder, Miriam was captivated with the patterns of purple, royal blue and scarlet in the developing design. She noted that it was at times of stress that her mistress would weave. It soothed her nerves.

Miriam gathered her courage like strings on a loom and tiptoed towards her.

"Mistress?" she called softly.

Adara was deep in thought again. She hardly noticed Miriam.

The girl spoke a bit louder. "Ma'am?"

The woman shook from her dreamlike state and turned to look into Miriam's tender eyes. She found compassion there.

"I think I know someone who could help."

The mistress tilted her head, furrowing her brow with a frown. "Help with—?"

"With Master Naaman's leprosy."

"But how? How could you know someone who could help, being so far from home?"

"This one I am speaking of lives back in Samaria. Near my home town."

"What could a mere man do that even our gods cannot do?" Adara said bitterly.

"He has power from our Mighty One—Jehovah. He brought a boy back to life many years ago. But it wasn't his power. It was our Almighty Abba's. Our Father in Heaven above."

Adara stared at Miriam, trying to take it all in. Finally, sitting upright, she spoke.

"What is this man's name and title? Where will I find him? How will I send him a message?"

"He is the prophet Elisha. And he lives in Israel. I do not know where he is at this moment, but he is well-known. Even the king of Israel knows of his deeds and prophecies."

The mistress rose instantly to her feet.

"This might save our darling daughter. I will speak to Naaman at once!"

Adara left in haste, without another word.

Maybe. Oh, Abba Father. I hope so. I want it to be so—let this be the answer!

CHAPTER SEVENTEEN

MIRIAM LET OUT A DEEP breath and skipped to the well to gather water for the day's duties, thinking about the possibilities. About miracles and wonders. The sun shined steady, no clouds hiding its brilliance today.

She did not mind the heaviness of the clay pots or the way the base dug into her shoulders. *When you have hope, you have everything.* She sang a little song her mother would sing as she went about her day—about Jehovah surrounding her in the trees above. In the mud between her toes. And the bird's sweet songs. *Life is good. No, life is beautiful. Life is a sweet, sweet song today.*

Returning to the house, Miriam saw the master and his wife leaving together in the chariot. This was an unusual thing. Miriam knew it would be impolite to ask. *Still . . .*

She made her way carefully towards the kitchen, lost in thought, trying not to spill the water. Barely able to see around the jug, she swerved, narrowly missed a figure walking towards her in the hallway.

Miriam blurted out, "Oh, Jamal, sorry—I didn't see you there." The boy chuckled and stopped alongside her, steadying the jug in her arms. Her curiosity got the better of her. "I—I saw the mistress and master leaving just now. Do you know where they are headed?"

"The master has requested a meeting with the king of Syria. His name is Ben-Hadad. He and the mistress have gone to the palace to dine. Why are you so interested, little maid?" Jamal's eyes beamed as the corners of his lips turned upward.

"I, well—I was just wondering. That's all." Miriam looked down, concentrating on a crack in the floor, feeling the weight of the jug.

"Ah, I see. Let me help you with this jug," he said, taking it from her. Turning towards the kitchen he added, "then, why don't you come with me to check on the animals? I need to remind the stable boy to lay fresh grass in the stalls. I could use a friend to keep me company."

Miriam glanced up and hesitated. Would she be in trouble if she left her daily duties for a short while? Hands resting on his hips, Jamal waited for an answer. She grinned and thought how much like a big brother he looked and acted. Remembering she had completed her morning chores, she finally answered.

"Alright. I suppose it couldn't hurt."

They walked together down the well-worn path to the stable. Lifting her face to the morning sun, she took pleasure in its warming rays. Joy sprang up in her soul. She had found someone to talk to. Someone who cared.

As they entered, Miriam breathed in the freshly dried grasses which the small, disheveled boy was bundling and stacking along the stone wall. The donkey, horses, goats, and sheep were out in the fields, leaving their stalls empty for cleaning. This was the perfect time for outdoor tasks. Hot, dry afternoons made everyone—man and beast—ready for a nap.

Miriam turned her attention now to the older boy, who was becoming more to her than just another servant. She wanted to know more about him.

"How did you come to work in this household, Jamal?"

"My father was one of Master Naaman's trusted soldiers. That is, until he was struck down in battle."

Miriam sat on a low wooden stool and studied her dusty sandals. "Oh, I'm sorry. That must have been hard."

"Not really. I was just a babe. Soon after, my mother died of a terrible fever. She wouldn't eat and wasted away to nothing. So Master Naaman took me into his household and gave me a respectable position. I oversee the care of his animals, carts, carriages, and, most importantly, his chariot." Miriam saw the pride in his squared shoulders and wide smile.

"Then we are both orphans, you and I. Aren't we?" she said.

"Yes, you could say that. Although the master and mistress do love and care for me as their own."

Not exactly, thought Miriam. *They didn't choose him as the sacrifice to appease their idols for the master's leprosy. And I am glad.*

Miriam liked Jamal. He was kind. Thoughtful. And he was a good friend. In a strange place, it was necessary to have a good friend.

CHAPTER EIGHTEEN

MIRIAM DIDN'T HEAR THE MASTER and his wife come home that night. She was fast asleep, dreaming of home. The way it used to be. She saw their fields and vineyard and smelled her ima's flatbread and homemade goat's cheese. She heard the whimpering of little Zacchaeus and the lambs baaing in the corral. Sounds of donkeys braying, birds twittering, and abba whittling filled her visions.

He made such beautiful furniture. The entire village owned a piece of his hand-sculpted creations. But more than that, her abba was wise.

"We do not know what is in store for each of us, Miriam. But we do know, good or bad, it will work out for the best. Jehovah always puts us where our light shines the brightest. And, wherever that is, He is with us. Watching us. Loving us. How can we not love and obey Him in return?"

Miriam awoke in the dark with these thoughts on her heart. *Is my light shining so far from home?* More likely, it was under a bushel for none to see. She curled up under her sheepskin and waited for the dawn.

In the morning, Phoebe asked Miriam to bring the master and mistress their breakfast: fresh goat's cheese and some newly-picked fruit from their orchards to begin the day. She eagerly obeyed, hoping she wouldn't appear meddlesome.

In Tishri, the harvest month and time of high holy days, the master hired vinedressers to pick the ripe, plump, deep purple fruit from the grapevines and make wine. But it was not a drink to be served early in the day. And, of course, this household knew nothing of the holy days Yahweh had ordained for His people. Their celebrations, Miriam was sure, were all dancing and drinking with no thought of the Maker of all the universe.

Miriam quietly served them, carefully listening to the conversation between the two, who were stretched out on either side of a long wooden table. She returned to her position at the arched doorway, watching her master examine his arms and hands.

"Our great king Ben-Hadad has sent a letter to the king of Israel, asking him for help in finding a cure for my diseased skin. We must wait now for the outcome. Two, maybe three, days, and we will have our answer. Then, I will travel to Samaria."

"You cannot go alone, dear. I will go with you," Adara said, drawing herself up.

"Nonsense! I have my faithful servant Ahmad with me. He accompanied me in many battles. This one is no different."

Adara reached across the table and clasped his hand in hers, ignoring the white patches on them. "But Naaman—please. Let me go with you. I want to see that strange land Miriam has been telling me about. I want to thank him for his help."

"And ride on those bumpy roads? In this heat? I cannot let my wife do that." Naaman shook her hand away, glancing again at the flaws on his skin.

Adara got up from her reclining position, this time, grabbing his garment in protest.

"I would be willing, my dear. It would be a welcome adventure. So, you MUST let me go with you."

"Let us see what the morning brings. I will not go until the king of Israel responds. Tomorrow will tell."

Miriam rested her head against the cool stone wall. Things were moving much too fast for her. *Could the king of Israel truly help?* Healing the people under his control was not a responsibility of a king. Only Jehovah held that power. *Yes, I wonder what tomorrow will bring for my master.* Drop by drop, Miriam's anxious heart was melting.

CHAPTER NINETEEN

"IS HE MAD?! WHO DOES he think he is?" said the commander.

"Naaman, my dear, it does seem like a strange request, but it is not a difficult one." Adara placed her hands on Naaman's broad chest, then, quickly removed them. He continued his rampage:

"But we have rivers—pristine rivers; two, I might add, just a few miles from here. Why do I need to wash in the Jordan? It's filthy! The task is not befitting someone of my rank."

He turned from his wife, burying his head in his hands. Already she could see the pale blotches spreading on his skin. She shuddered, and continued their conversation, hoping to persuade him.

"Perhaps they do things differently in Samaria. The Israelites are a bit odd you know. Or maybe their God requires it. It's part of their land. Their history."

By this time, Miriam was hanging on to every word the pair spoke having stopped at the doorway to listen on her way to the kitchen. *What could it mean?* She moved into the room, positioning herself behind a palm tree growing to one side of the courtyard.

"I have heard that prophets are odd fellows, Naaman. They request strange things. Maybe Miriam could enlighten us." She raised her voice to call. "Miriam. MIRIAM!"

The girl stepped out from behind the tree immediately and made her presence known.

"Yes, Mistress?"

"Oh. I didn't see you there. Were you—Ummmm, never mind. Miriam, tell us. Do prophets request odd things of people?"

"I don't understand. What do you mean?" Miriam felt small in the presence of Adara and her commander-husband.

"Finally, after three days, King Ben-Hadad has heard from your king—of Israel. And he has received communication from the prophet Elisha. He is requesting that my husband go to Samaria. He claims if your master washes in the Jordan River seven times, he will be healed." Adara waited, wide-eyed, for a response.

"Yes, mistress—whatever the prophet requires, no matter how strange, the master must do. When he healed the widow's son near our village, he laid his body on top of the boy—hand to hand, feet to feet. He prayed, and breathed life into the boy's mouth. Is it so difficult a journey that he cannot obey Elisha's request?"

Adara looked at Naaman for an answer. "We have the means to go," she said with confidence.

The commander was silent, his brows furrowed. He rubbed his stubbly chin, as if it would respond for him.

Miriam continued. "If I had a disease, and the prophet made a request of me, I would do it immediately. His words and deeds never fail because his power is from Yahweh above." She raised her hands, hoping her prayers made it further than the ceiling.

"That settles it then," Adara said with a decisive tone. "Naaman," she pleaded as she knelt before her husband, "We must go. We must—it's your only hope."

The master pivoted and left the room with determined steps.

Miriam, unsure of the outcome, turned towards the door to leave. "Miriam?"

"Yes mistress?" She glanced back.

"Would you be willing to accompany us? Since you know this man Elisha, it would be well for you to go."

Miriam's breath caught in her throat. Her eyes brightened, not believing what she just heard. "Why, yes, Mistress! I would be happy to go. Thank you. I would be honored."

She felt like bursting. To be going home to Samaria! To her little village of Shunem. Was it possible? Could it be that her loved ones were still alive? *Maybe the prophet has some news of my family.* It would truly be a miracle if it were so. She shook her head, as if awaking from a dream. *Is this real?*

CHAPTER TWENTY

IN THE MORNING, THE HOUSE was buzzing. Adara gave orders right and left.

"Jamal, are the horses clean and fed? What about the carts—and the chariot?"

"Yes, Mistress. I will polish the brass until it gleams. By the ninth hour, when the sun is in the west, they will all be ready."

"Good." The mistress turned to one of her two servant girls. "And Rana?" The girl's eyes blinked rapidly as bodies rushed to and fro around her, making it difficult to concentrate on Mistress Adara's orders.

"Yes, Mistress?"

"The spices and herbs are drying on the rooftop. Wrap them with sisal in bundles and place them on the cart."

"Immediately, Mistress Adara." She bowed slightly then began her tasks with a light step.

"—and Miriam? Are the silks ready? And the woven cloths? What about the fine coats and coverings?" Adara asked checking off the items with her raised fingers.

"Yes, ma'am. They are in the chest ready to go." Miriam couldn't take her eyes off the mistress. She had never seen her in such a frenzy.

Adara called into the kitchen. "Phoebe!"

"Yes?" came the robust voice.

"Have you finished the candied walnuts? And what about the pastries? Are the goat-skins filled with the finest of our vineyard?" The mistress pushed away a stray hair from her beady forehead.

"Yes, Ma'am. They are wrapped in palm leaves. Where would you like them?" asked Phoebe.

"Stack them over there." She pointed to an open chest on the floor nearby, neatly packed by Miriam's careful hands.

"Yes—right away," said the cook.

On and on the requests were made and tasks accomplished. Soon, it was time to leave.

First, Naaman and his choice servant Ahmad rode in the chariot leading the entourage. Then, a few carts with foods and spices. Following, was the carriage with Mistress Adara, and her young maid, Miriam. Lastly, carts laden with clothing trailed behind with two soldiers at the end to protect the lot from would-be attackers.

Miriam glanced back at Rana, who smiled shyly and waved, seemingly if she was willing to let her friend go. *I will miss her. What a change. Miracles still do happen.*

Phoebe and Jamal stood alongside Rana, their hands in the air as a parting gesture. Miriam returned the farewell, and then faced forward in the direction of destiny. *I will miss them. Very much. They have become dear to me.* She reflected on that thought for a moment. *What a wonder that Gentiles would become a part of my life. Jehovah was full of surprises!*

They rode back through Damascus and down the bustling street called Straight. People, young and old, cheered them as they passed by, stopping their haggling and conversations to hail their brave warrior once more. Only this time he faced another deadly enemy—leprosy. News had traveled fast—the commander had found a potential cure.

How different things seemed since the first time she laid eyes on this city. Even her bitter heart had changed!

Miriam gazed up at the tall pillars on either side of the cobbled roadway as they passed through the Damascus gate. It made her quite dizzy. She remembered entering this gate weeks before. It seemed strange and imposing at the time. Now, they appeared magnificent. *Am I really traveling alongside my mistress, and are we truly on our way back to my hometown?*

She pinched her arm slightly, just to make sure she wasn't dreaming. Had Jehovah answered her prayers? Only He knew what lay ahead. Would her master grant her freedom for a cure? Or, would he refuse to wash in the Jordan once he arrived? If so, she would be dragged back again. Then their precious daughter would be sacrificed.

No. No use worrying. It is too soon to tell.

CHAPTER TWENTY-ONE

THEY CONTINUED THEIR JOURNEY UNTIL close to sunset, traveling south, away from the verdant hills and well-watered land. The day had been hot and dry, but the carriage had a cover, which shielded them from the blazing sun. Miriam was fascinated with the wildlife in the Syrian Desert. She spotted foxes and wolves roaming the landscape, and occasional flocks of gazelles, reminding her of Vashti. She didn't want to think of that refined yet nimble girl's fate if the prophet could not cure her master. *If?* She was ashamed of her lack of faith in Elisha's healing power. The graceful gazelle mesmerized her—its sleekness and sure-footedness. She wished she could be as beautiful as that creature. Instead, she felt clumsy and boyish.

When they stopped for a rest, she watched with interest the snakes and lizards crawling on the parched earth alongside their carriage.

"Oh, mistress! Look at that odd little creature with the spiny covering. I've never seen such an animal."

"Ah, yes—the lowly hedgehog. Rather curious in habit. When frightened, he rolls into a prickly ball for protection. And, what's more, the creature is resistant to snake venom."

What an awesome Creator we have. Miriam wasn't sure if it was the time to say it out loud.

As darkness set in, they soon found an oasis surrounded by a ring of palms. The servants put up the goat skin and heavy cloth tents for the night, placing wool blankets and pillows inside for comfort.

The men, including Naaman, would sleep outside, taking turns to guard the women.

After a simple meal of dried fish, flatbread, olives and dates, they warmed themselves before the brush fire. Later, Adara and Miriam settled underneath the sheepskins in their tent. Miriam could feel the night wrapping its arms around her. The cool air raised the flesh on her arms. As her mistress was about to blow out the olive oil lantern, she spoke.

"My dear?"

"Yes, Mistress?" Miriam stared intently at her somber face, watching reflected shadows from the lamp play over her high cheekbones.

"Even if we are unsuccessful tomorrow, I will not hold you accountable. You are just a girl, not yet thirteen—and you have done your best."

She cupped Miriam's chin in her cool hands as she spoke. *She reminds me of my ima sometimes.* Now was one of those times.

Miriam let out a sigh. She hadn't realized how tense she was, worried this would not work out—that her master would not be healed. She smiled momentarily at Adara, then her eyes began to fill with tears.

"Yes, Mistress. Thank you, Mistress." Miriam wiped the dampness from her cheek.

Even with these words of assurance, she still prayed. *Oh, Master of the Impossible and Divider of the sea, hear my prayer. Lead us to the holy prophet so my master might be healed.*

Miriam stopped short, not believing what was about to come into her mind—*Whether it means my freedom or not . . .*

Her cold, stubborn heart kept on melting with the setting sun, a tear at a time.

CHAPTER TWENTY-TWO

ANOTHER DAY DAWNED BRIGHTLY, BUT, to a certain girl, its brilliance wasn't caused by the sun. It was bright with possibilities. After a simple breakfast of hummus, dates, and goat's cheese, the caravan packed up and continued towards Samaria, bumping along on the uneven roads. Miriam closed her eyes and thought of the low hills, covered with Cyprus trees and golden thistle, dotting the landscape back home.

She remembered an encounter with the prophet Elisha. He, like Elijah before him, was staying with a widow woman in an upper room of her tiny clay home in their hometown near Jezreel.

During that time, Miriam's mother had lost another child, the year before her brother Zacchaeus was born. Her mind went back to that season of sorrow, recalling Elisha's words as he fixed his eyes on her troubled face.

"What ails you, young one?" the prophet asked.

"My mother's baby—m-my sister—did not survive. Ima is worn out and grieving, and I am, too."

"Jehovah gives, and He takes away. We do not know His will, but we must be content with it."

The prophet spoke without removing his gaze. Miriam called to mind those piercing brown eyes and wild, flowing gray hair. Although he did not embrace her, she felt Elisha's comfort none the less.

In another memory, she was sitting beside her friend Jonas, the widow's son. Elisha had brought *him* back to life with the power of Jehovah. Why not her newborn sister? It didn't seem fair. Jehovah took *their* baby but gave *back* the widow's son.

Would the Almighty take my master's health and livelihood away? Or return it with a miracle? Has the Almighty taken my family instead?

Returning to the present, Miriam watched two vultures in the distance tearing apart a camel's carcass. Death. Death of home, dreams, and self. She was feeling it more and more as the day wore on, the heat bearing down on their chain of camels, carts, and carriages.

But, as the terrain changed from desert to lush rolling hills, her spirits lifted. The brilliant red of corn poppies came into view along with tiny white narcissus with yellow centers and delicate blue lupine. Miriam took a deep pleasurable breath of Galilean air blown in from the sea. She felt the moisture in it. It revived her. *It's looking more like home. Home.* Just thinking the word filled her with joy. The corners of her mouth turned gently upward, as if pulled by an unseen thread. By the end of the day, they would arrive in Samaria. What would she find there?

Adara studied Miriam's face as the carriage continued its course south towards its destination. Jolting and rocking as it went along, it brought an almost comforting rhythm to the journey.

"What are you pondering, dear? You look deep in thought again."

By now, Miriam felt comfortable answering these types of questions. They did not threaten her as they did before. She had come to trust in her mistress.

"I'm—well— I'm worried about what I might discover when we arrive. What if I can't find my parents? What if they are dead? And, baby Zacchaeus—I can't bear to think of it."

Adara wrapped her arm gently around the girl's shoulder, pulling her close. As her head rested on her chest, Miriam could smell the cinnamon and rose wafting from Adara's hair. It lifted her spirits. She relaxed and closed her weary eyes.

"Even though I do not believe in your God, Miriam, I can sense that He is watching you. That His hand is upon you. And He has plans for you. I never thought I would say that about a god, but your God is not one made of stone or wood. He is one who hears and cares deeply. He is a God who sees."

Miriam's eyelids shot open. That last phrase made Miriam start. A story rekindled in her mind. One she had long forgotten.

"That is exactly what Hagar, the handmaiden of Sarah said to Jehovah when she fled into the desert with her son, Ishmael. He was sent away by Abraham the patriarch with no inheritance. But still, our Jehovah looked after her." Miriam let out a sigh, basking in the peace she felt at that moment.

"And so, He will look after you, Miriam. I know it."

The mistress gazed out at the rolling hills, now turning dark green and bronze as the afternoon sun advanced towards the horizon. Miriam studied her silhouette, watching crinkles forming around Adara's eyes as she softly smiled. She wanted to hold this memory in her heart for a very long time.

CHAPTER TWENTY-THREE

SOON HER VILLAGE OF SHUNEM came into view. The caravan entered the marketplace, passing a few merchant stalls selling cloth, spices, animals, and clay pots. Nothing like the busy place she remembered. Miriam sat up, straining her neck to see over the edge of the carriage. Both grief and rage welled up within her heart as she witnessed the tell-tale signs of the Syrian conquest. No—her master's conquest. Ragged tent coverings, singed wooden carts, and tumbled and broken pillars met her gaze. Her eyes scanned the stalls.

Could they possibly still be here? Selling in the marketplace? Miriam let out a gasp. As her eyes scanned the scene, she noticed the cart which held their herbs and spices on market day. It lay overturned and broken. Even worse, she thought she saw blood stains on the white awning, which now was ripped and ragged.

"No! It can't be!"

Adara shifted immediately in her seat. "What is it Miriam? What did you see?"

"Our stall. It's. Not. There." Her heart began to race, as tears flowed freely down her cheeks.

"But, there might be another answer. Possibly they've moved?" Miriam was drawn by her mistress's compassionate eyes. But still, she was losing hope quickly.

"Never. They would *never* leave their home." Miriam brushed a tear with the back of her hand.

The caravan continued through the village and on south to the outskirts of Samaria where the king's grand residence was located. Miriam scanned the road for a familiar face. *Maybe the mistress is right— could they have fled to Samaria for shelter?*

They stopped in front of the palace with its towering white-washed walls and impressive stairway leading to a set of massive doors carved with images of lions and eagles.

Naaman dismounted his chariot and adjusted his red tunic and gold breastplate and helmet, dressed once again as a mighty warrior. Motioning his servant, Ahmad, to pick up a wooden box from the covered cart, he complied, handing it to the commander. Miriam watched as he walked up the flight of stairs leading to the column-flanked entrance. *The master looks so small. How can a mighty man seem so insignificant?* Miriam had questions.

"Where is the master going with that box?"

Adara's lips curved into a gentle smile.

"I have it on good authority that my husband is bringing a letter from our own King Ben-Hadad to your king of Israel, asking for healing. And, of course, he has brought plenty of gifts in payment."

Miriam's brow furrowed, her eyes large and searching. "But, it is not the king, mistress, who will heal him. It is the prophet Elisha. *He* has the power from on high."

Adara motioned towards the palace. "It is customary in our culture to address the king first. Ben-Hadad wanted it that way."

Miriam nodded slowly and then looked back the way they had come, hoping to find anyone from Shunem town, but she found none. Miriam shivered as a sudden chilling thought came to her. *What if everyone I knew in my town has been killed or captured?*

Miriam shot up from her seat in the carriage when she spotted a familiar striped tunic out of the corner of her eye.

She opened her mouth to shout his name, but the young man disappeared before she could release his name into the arid wind. *Jonas!* He was the big brother she had always wanted. Being born to a childless couple was the first miracle. Being raised from the dead by the prophet was the second miracle. It would be *thrice* a miracle if he had fought the Syrian army and survived.

She was brought back to reality when she heard arguing at the front of the caravan. Turning, Miriam was puzzled to see her master madly waving his arms at his servant, words spewing from his lips. He was too far away for Miriam to catch the conversation. *Was there trouble?*

CHAPTER TWENTY-FOUR

THE STORY WAS DELIVERED SOON enough to Mistress Adara. The king of Israel, after reading the Syrian king's letter, ripped his clothing in great distress.

"I have no power to heal! This is a trick meant to lead us into war. There is no resolution," he was heard to say.

But then, miraculously, the prophet Elisha, who was there witnessing the event, spoke thus: "You may not have the power, oh, King, but our Jehovah indeed has. Tell him to come to my home this day, and he will be healed." Then, he rushed out before Naaman could address the prophet.

This was welcome news for Miriam. Could that be why she saw Jonas in town? Was Elisha still living with Jonas and his parents? *He might have news of my family!* Miriam knew how Jonas greatly loved the prophet. She snapped to attention when the caravan began its journey once again, traveling down another road in the city where most of its inhabitants lived.

On the way, she passed her close friend Jochebed's home. Memories of playing at the river's edge flooded her mind and just as quickly disappeared when Miriam noticed the broken wheels, crumbling stone fence, and slashed door of the home. *Not her, too!* She willed away a tear. *Is there no one left to greet me?*

The local carpenter was nowhere to be seen, but Miriam surveyed his shop as they passed. It seemed in good repair. Feelings of anger raised their haunches, ready to fight. *Why couldn't it have been the carpenter instead? Why?* She consciously began to resist the impulse to complain. War must not be fought with the Most High. One could never win. *And besides,* Miriam thought to herself, *Jehovah does as He wills. He is not a man that I can contend with.*

Passing a few more run-down homes built of stone, they came to the end of the way. There, on the left, was the humble whitewashed abode, standing surprisingly intact.

The caravan made quite a stir. By the time it had reached Elisha's home, a few villagers, young and old, came from behind the rubble. They stared curiously, mouths hinged open as if catching flies. The noise of a multitude of hoofed animals would draw attention, let alone the procession of richly decorated carts and carriages. Would they recognize the man responsible for their loss?

Naaman's trusted servant Ahmad jumped from his beast of burden and knocked at the door. It was minutes before it slowly opened. A medium height muscular man with flowing grey hair and beard appeared. His face seemed flushed.

The prophet must have been on his knees praying. Miriam remembered well watching him bow his head to the ground as he petitioned Jehovah.

The servant spoke to the prophet, and immediately returned to address the commander. The discussion became heated. Each man's gestures and facial expressions moved faster and more intense as the conversation went on. *I'm truly thankful I am not a man. They always seem to be in conflict in words and war.*

Just then, Miriam noticed the boy in the striped tunic. She opened her mouth once again to call out to Jonas, but he moved out of sight as Naaman's servant made his way back towards Adara's carriage. She stood and spoke as he came alongside the carriage.

"What is the problem?"

The servant's face crinkled and pulled as he spoke. "The prophet has reminded the master of his request to have him wash seven times in the Jordan River nearby. He claims it will cleanse his body of the leprosy. He cannot speak to the master directly until he is purified from the disease. But, as you might have guessed, once again, the master refuses. He claims there are many unpolluted rivers at home where he could carry out the task."

"Please," Adara pleaded, "bring my husband to me."

"Yes, ma'am."

He left to do her bidding, just as a friendly voice broke into the tense scene.

"Miriam? Is it really you? How—"

Miriam turned. "Jonas. You're safe! And what about—"

Naaman approached their carriage, his head down, hands on his forehead, cutting off all hopes of conversation for the moment. He looked up at his wife, shielding his eyes from the sun's rays.

"You wanted to speak with me?"

Adara waited, choosing her words carefully.

"Do your soldiers trust you to make wise decisions?"

Naaman's brow furrowed in confusion. "What does this have to do with my healing?"

"Just answer me, Naaman."

"Yes, of course. They know that I have had many years of experience and have won many battles. They trust me. And they obey." His face loosened suddenly.

Adara continued, "This prophet Elisha has performed miracles through his God for many years. My maid, Miriam, has been telling me about them. Would it be such a hardship to obey this man? Do you truly want to be healed? Please, my dear. Just follow his leading. Obey his request."

Naaman looked from his wife to Miriam, and back again. He was drawn in by the girl's sweet, endearing face. It begged him to act.

"For you, my sweet wife, I will do it. But I do not relish muddy water. It is beneath my status to wash in such a place."

"The muddy water will turn sweet if in the process, it heals." Adara's mouth curved upward, as if cajoling.

The commander's eyes fixed on his wife in admiration. They glistened, speaking volumes. He approached Ahmad once more to reply. Miriam and her mistress watched from afar as Elisha stood before Naaman, raised his hands and bowed his head to pray.

Leaving the carts full of gold, silver, and fine clothes behind with the servants, the two main carriages left for the Jordan, only a few miles away. As the horses jolted forward, again the familiar voice called out.

"Psssst. Miriam!"

As soon as she caught his eye, Jonas smiled and mouthed the words she so longed to hear:

They—are—safe.

Joy mingled with hope filled Miriam's heart as they traveled towards the muddy Jordan. *I'm in the middle of something big. A grand plan.* Miriam's mind hurt with the thoughts.

CHAPTER TWENTY-FIVE

THE CARAVAN MEANDERED THROUGH A tall grove of oak, willow and tamarisk trees, cooling the air and shading the travelers from the end of the summer sun. Their roots sank deep into the ground, drawing water from the Jordan. Miriam's gaze wandered to the sky, noticing a bird of prey gliding above the treetops, its eyes scanning the ground for a meal. Alongside the carriage, scrub bushes appeared on either side the road sheltering lizards and snakes that would sometimes scurry across.

As they moved forward, Miriam could see the river's edge coming into view. The trees were sparse here opening to the gently flowing river, now shallow after the blazing days of the hot season. Thickets of reeds, scrub, and stones lined the banks of the muddy green water. Adara and Miriam watched with pleasure as marsh frogs, salamanders, and soft-shelled turtles played along the banks, sunning themselves on a stone or thick branch jutting from the Jordan.

When the carriage stopped, Miriam attempted to stand, ready to alight, but a hand pulled her back.

"No, dear. Stay. The commander would not wish women to observe him washing in this filthy water. It is enough to know he is willing. Let's save his pride, Miriam. We can see clearly from where we are." Adara was firm but kind.

Miriam was disappointed but understood pride. She amused herself, watching a hoopoe bird sporting a tall crown of feathers, pecking the ground with its long narrow beak, looking for a morsel to eat. Her mind went back to another river bank years ago where she stood her ground against Jonas as they played along a branch of the Jordan outside of town.

"Boys don't *always* win," she remembered saying. "I'm just as strong. I can use a sling with the best of them!" Miriam prided herself in saying so. And it *was* true. But the best truth was this: her family was *alive!* Praise Jehovah of the Heavens.

The splashing of water brought Miriam back to reality as she watched the commander from afar. She could see the outline of his broad bare shoulders, large head and muscle-laden arms. *The ones that took innocent lives.* The stubborn old Miriam was returning. She was amazed at how quickly that happened. *We so easily stray from our Jehovah.* She remembered Elisha's words just days before Naaman's army left her beloved village in ruins.

Adara and Miriam sat without a word, as they focused intently on the scene before them, squinting and shielding their eyes from the sun.

Once, twice, thrice.

Each time Naaman rose from the dirty Jordan, he examined his arms and chest. Four, five, six times. He dipped with no apparent change.

Miriam held her breath as she waited for the master to break the surface of the water for the seventh time. It seemed like an eternity. Unlike the other times, this time, when he rose, he stood still. No movement or gestures.

Adara and Miriam rose as one from the carriage, standing perfectly still—waiting.

"Can you see anything, mistress?"

Just then, they heard a wild shout as Naaman's hands raised to the sky. He spun around and around, forcing waves to the shore.

Decorum or not, the two climbed out of the carriage and made haste towards the master. Miriam, a swift runner, arrived first. Naaman reached out to grasp a towel from his servant's hand but turned as he heard someone cry out.

"It's a miracle!" shouted Adara, catching up to Miriam. "The holy prophet's words are true—you are healed. The prophet Elisha has healed Naaman!" Then she did something she had wanted to do for weeks—she dashed into the water and embraced her husband. Miriam and Ahmad cheered, jumping and shouting with glee. Naaman's strong arms encircled his wife, their forms swaying in a silent dance. Miriam's heart melted in a puddle at her feet. "It is our God, Jehovah, who has healed him. Praise be to Jehovah our Father!"

Joy burst from her soul. Miriam knew yet another healing had taken place—and it was more than skin deep.

EPILOGUE: THE REST OF THE STORY . . .

IT WAS TRUE. MIRIAM'S HEART had changed—by the very One who made her. The Creator who had made *all* things. The One who knew Miriam inside and out and could make all things work together for good, no matter what. God chose to protect her family, so they could be re-united. And miracle of miracles, Naaman was instrumental in this process. He found them and offered them shelter and work under his roof and protection. And, slowly but surely, Naaman's household learned of the Almighty God, Creator of the heavens and earth. Jehovah-Jireh. The God who provides.

Miriam and her family learned to forgive those who had harmed them. They accepted what God had planned. All that befell them, good and bad, was filtered through His fingers of love. But even if He hadn't brought her family back to Miriam, God still would have been good. For this life is not the end of all things. In His time, God will make it all right in the end.

And the best part? This very same God is present today. He is nearby—waiting. And watching. And loving. For He is the Heart Changer.

Dear Reader: If you were blessed by this book and want to share it with others, consider writing a review on Amazon, Goodreads, Christian books, and Barnes and Noble websites. Or, give a copy to your public, church, or Christian school library. I'd love to keep in touch with my readers. Sign up for my email list at www.jarmdelboccio.com.

May your heart grow warmer as you draw closer to the Heart Changer . . .

Author's Note

I have always had a soft spot for children in the Bible who have no name or backstory. Only God knows what happened to them after a miraculous encounter with the Almighty. But, I can imagine, can't I?

Miriam is one of those characters. Giving her a name and a backstory is my way of making history and the Bible come alive for my readers. That is my passion.

The true account of Miriam (not her real name) can be found in the Old Testament in 2 Kings 5. Read it for yourself!

Of course, it tells us nothing about Miriam, other than the fact she was a maid captured from Israel and was instrumental in bringing Elisha the prophet and Naaman the commander of the Syrian army together.

Naaman's wife is mentioned in title only, without a name, so I took the liberty to develop her character fully, which included the couple's relationship. The servants are all fictitious, as are the soldiers.

It is possible Miriam lived close to Elisha's town in Samaria, which is how she would have known of his miracles. And of course, the widow and her son (Miriam's friend, Jonas) would have lived nearby.

I have attempted to remain faithful to the text with the professions, faith and personalities of Elisha and Naaman, writing their dialogue and descriptions in keeping with the biblical account.

Using many online sources, I attempted to describe the setting as best as I could, with help from friends who live in that part of the world. Although some animals and plants might no longer be in existence, it is a strong possibility they were present in the 9th century BC.

Since Syria bordered Israel in those days, and the two nations were often at war, most officials, tradesmen, and wealthy adults would have had an understanding of Aramaic (their own language) and Hebrew, since they came from the same roots. Miriam and the other servants in Naaman's household would have been able to communicate on a basic level. But, to move the story along without confusion and disruption, I let the reader assume they were fluent in each other's mother tongue. This is a historical fiction author's right.

I trust I have not been offensive in any way to the Hebrew culture, which is why I asked a knowledgeable friend for advice.

The last verse of the hymn, "The Love of God," composed by Frederick Martin Lehman, uses an excerpt from the poem "Akdamut" by Jewish poet, Rabbi Meir Ben Isaac Nehorai, 1050 A.D.:

"Could we with ink the ocean fill,
    And were the skies of parchment made;
Were every stalk on earth a quill,
    And every man a scribe by trade;
To write the love of God above
    Would drain the ocean dry;
Nor could the scroll contain the whole,
    Though stretched from sky to sky."

THE
HEART
CHANGER
Teacher's Guide

AVAILABLE ONLINE AT
WWW.AMBASSADOR-INTERNATIONAL.COM

For more information about
Jarm Del Boccio
&
The Heart Changer
please visit:

www.jarmdelboccio.com
www.facebook.com/JarmDelBoccio
@JarmVee
www.instagram.com/jarmveedb

For more information about
AMBASSADOR INTERNATIONAL
please visit:

www.ambassador-international.com
@AmbassadorIntl
www.facebook.com/AmbassadorIntl

*If you enjoyed this book, please consider leaving us a review on
Amazon, Goodreads, or our website.*

www.ingramcontent.com/pod-product-compliance
Lightning Source LLC
Chambersburg PA
CBHW072009170626
46813CB00005B/2074